"What do you want, Riley?"

She lifted her chin and met his gaze. "A husband."

He stared at her a moment, as if he couldn't possibly have heard her right. Then he broke into laughter that began as a quiet chuckle and escalated to a deep belly laugh that had him nearly doubled over.

"You've got jokes, I see, princess." He wiped his eyes, still laughing. "For a hot second, I thought you might be serious."

"I am serious." Riley folded her arms. "You need a million dollars. I need a husband for one year."

"Rich people." Travis shook his head, as if he himself didn't fit that description. "You think the rules don't apply to you. That you can do whatever the hell you want. I'm not a mail-order husband, sweetheart. But I'm sure you can find yourself one for a lot less."

* * *

Just a Little Married by Reese Ryan is part of the Moonlight Ridge series.

Dear Reader,

The Moonlight Ridge trilogy, set in Asheville, North Carolina, follows the romantic adventures of three adopted brothers who are former foster kids.

Once close, the brothers drifted apart in the wake of a life-altering car accident. When the health of their adoptive father and the future of his livelihood is in jeopardy, the estranged brothers rally together to help the man who means everything to them and save the mountain resort where they grew up.

In *Just a Little Married*, celebrity chef Travis Holloway returns to Moonlight Ridge to upgrade the resort's questionable cuisine and make Moonlight Ridge a can't-miss culinary destination. When his ex, investment heiress Riley George, makes a proposal that will solve the resort's money problems and help him realize his dream of opening a signature restaurant on the property, he finds himself saying *I do*. But can their temporary marriage of convenience turn into something real?

Visit reeseryan.com/desirereaders to share your questions or comments on the trilogy or drop me a line. While you're there, join my VIP Readers newsletter list for book news, giveaways and more.

Reese Ryan

REESE RYAN

———

JUST A LITTLE MARRIED

HARLEQUIN

DESIRE

Recycling programs
for this product may
not exist in your area.

ISBN-13: 978-1-335-73519-5

Just a Little Married

This edition published by arrangement with Harlequin Books S.A.

For questions and comments about the quality of this book, please contact us at CustomerService@Harlequin.com.

Harlequin Enterprises ULC
22 Adelaide St. West, 40th Floor
Toronto, Ontario M5H 4E3, Canada
www.Harlequin.com

Printed in U.S.A.

Reese Ryan writes sexy, emotional romance with captivating family drama, surprising secrets and complicated characters.

A panelist at the 2017 Los Angeles Times Festival of Books and recipient of the 2020 Donna Hill Breakout Author Award, Reese is an advocate for the romance genre and diversity in fiction.

Connect with Reese via Facebook, Twitter, Instagram or reeseryan.com. Join her VIP Readers Lounge at bit.ly/VIPReadersLounge. Check out her YouTube show, where romance readers and authors connect at bit.ly/ReeseRyanChannel.

Books by Reese Ryan

Harlequin Desire

The Bourbon Brothers

Moonlight Ridge

Visit her Author Profile page at Harlequin.com, or reeseryan.com, for more titles.

You can find Reese Ryan on Facebook, along with other Harlequin Desire authors, at Facebook.com/harlequindesireauthors!

Thank you to Joss Wood, who came up with the idea for this fun trilogy and was gracious enough to invite me and Karen Booth along for the ride. Thank you, Karen, for wrangling the three of us and our ideas and for being a graphics genius who can always pull our disparate visions together.

Thank you to Tasha L. Harrison, K. Sterling, Meka James, Lisa Kessler and the entire Wordmakers group, who cheered me on every step of the way as I wrote and revised this book.

Thank you to the phenomenal readers in my Reese Ryan VIP Readers Lounge on Facebook. I'm ever grateful for your continued support.

A special thank-you to Angela Anderson, Stephanie Perkins and Shavonna Futrell, who were instrumental in helping to make my previous Harlequin Desire release—*Waking Up Married* (Bourbon Brothers #5)—a better book. Your loyal readership and honest feedback mean the world to me.

One

"Good to see you again, Chef Travis." The valet greeted Travis Holloway with a wide grin and held up a copy of Travis's latest cookbook. "Would you mind signing this for my girlfriend? She *loves* your competitive cooking show."

Travis was tired and groggy after a long night at his restaurant in Atlanta and a nearly four-hour drive to Asheville that morning. But he would always be gracious. He greeted the younger man warmly, signed the cookbook and suggested they take a selfie that would impress the man's girlfriend. Then he handed off the keys to his black Dodge Charger SRT Hellcat Widebody.

Once the valet drove away, Travis turned toward the building in front of him.

Moonlight Ridge.

Whenever he returned to the luxury resort, nestled in

the Blue Ridge Mountains, he couldn't help thinking of when he'd first seen it. He was seven. A social worker escorted him here, telling him how lucky he was that this estate would be his new home. And that his new "father" and "brothers" eagerly awaited his arrival.

His stomach tightened in a knot at seeing his brothers again now, just as it had that day twenty-six years ago.

After a long absence, Travis had first returned to Moonlight Ridge a few months earlier, because his adoptive father, Jameson Holloway, the owner of Moonlight Ridge, had suffered a brain episode. He and his adoptive brothers had been forced to come together, despite years of estrangement following a car accident that had changed all of their lives—his especially.

They'd committed to working together to oversee their father's at-home care and to help restore Moonlight Ridge, which had fallen into disrepair over the past decade. Over the past few months, his brothers, Mack and Grey, had taken the lead on overseeing the updates to the resort. They'd made vast improvements, but a lot still needed to be done.

The resort's food services needed an overhaul, and that was his area of expertise.

Travis climbed the stairs and entered the rotunda. Then he made his way up the grand staircase in the lobby. The elegant space still had many of its original architectural features and decor from when it was built in the 1930s. Travis glided his hand along the banister he and his brothers slid down as boys. He grinned, recalling that winter Mack had gotten the bright idea to sled down the stairwell.

It hadn't ended well.

Travis continued to the third floor, where the offices

were located. He stood in front of his father's office, the door partially ajar, and sighed.

Travis, Mack and Grey, all former foster kids, had all been a handful. Each of them was dealing with their own brand of family-induced trauma. It'd taken time, but the three of them had become brothers in every sense of the word. It was the Holloway brothers against the world.

Until it wasn't.

The night of the car accident that had changed everything would forever be burned into Travis's brain. It was the night his entire life went to shit. The night he'd lost his family and, for a time, the use of his legs. It was the night he'd lost his football scholarship, his dreams of playing in the NFL and the girl he'd believed he'd loved more than anything in the world.

It was the night he'd been reminded that there were few people he could trust implicitly. But his adoptive father, Jameson Holloway, sat atop that short list. He'd nursed him back to health, never allowing him to give up or feel sorry for himself. Always believing he would walk again, regardless of the grim initial diagnosis.

Like always, the old man was right. But it had taken him two grueling years to get there.

And though his body was whole again, he'd emerged from the entire ordeal irrevocably broken. He'd pushed his brothers away. Bitter over the loss of his dreams. Resentful that they'd come out of the accident unscathed, moving on with the lives they'd planned for themselves. Devastated over the girl whose betrayal had triggered everything that happened that horrible night. Angry with the world in general.

Through therapy, he'd worked out a lot of that anger. Since their father's illness, Travis had been forced to spend time with Mack and Grey in person and via phone and videoconferences. He'd been reestablishing a tentative relationship with his brothers. Partly out of a sense of obligation to their father. Partly out of his own guilt over how he'd handled the fallout from the accident.

He'd been wrong to blame his brothers, but he couldn't turn back time. Things would never be the same between them, so spending time with Mack and Grey in person still caused a knot in his gut. It was why he'd bailed immediately after Mack's wedding.

An emergency with the show had arisen, and Travis had taken the opportunity to delay his return. But now he was ready to get started. The sooner they got Moonlight Ridge running smoothly again, the sooner he could return to his life.

Travis entered the room and slipped into the seat beside Grey. "Sorry I'm late."

"Thought you'd changed your mind." Mack, who sat behind the desk, raised a brow. "I called. You didn't answer."

"I was on a call with a potential investor for the proposed New York restaurant." Travis imitated Mack's stern tone and cadence, causing Grey to chuckle. "But I'm here now."

Mack didn't find Travis's spot-on imitation amusing. His frown deepened. "Then let's get started. My *wife* is waiting."

"How is Molly?" Travis nodded toward the door between this adjoining office and hers.

He'd always liked Molly Haskell. Her father had worked at the resort, and Molly and Mack had been an item as teenagers. The relationship ended when Mack left, not long after the accident.

Travis was glad his brother and Molly had found their way back to each other. They belonged together. Not that he believed in soul mates or the sunshine-and-rainbows bullshit about love. Personal experience had taught him better than to believe that.

What he did believe in was mutually beneficial alliances. That was the best anyone could hope for in a relationship. And the relationship between Mack and Molly was equally beneficial. Or maybe sixty/forty was more accurate. After all, Mack "Know It All" Holloway could be a lot for anyone to deal with.

"She's doing well." A soft grin curved Mack's mouth.

For all of his alpha male posturing, Mack was a soft, gooey-in-the-center romantic. His brother had fallen in deep. If he didn't look so damn giddy—by Mack Holloway standards—Travis would feel sorry for him.

"She's meeting with our department heads. She'll stop by and give us an update, *if* we're ever done here," Mack groused. "I know you're living the bachelor life and you've got nothing but time, but our significant others have planned a double date for us, so…"

Travis felt a twinge of envy. Mack was newly married. Grey was deeply involved with Moonlight Ridge's wedding coordinator, Autumn Kincaid. When he'd seen his brothers at Mack and Molly's wedding two weeks earlier, both men seemed settled and happy.

But before the uneasy feeling could take hold, he reminded himself *the bachelor life* he was living was a pretty damn good one. One most men would be envious of.

He enjoyed glamorous events, luxury accommodations, extravagant vacations and designer gear—most of it on someone else's dime. And there was no shortage of beautiful women clamoring to be on his arm when he walked the red carpet at the opening of one of his restaurants or some social event. He had no reason to be envious of Mack or Grey.

His life was just fine the way it was.

"Then let's get down to business." Travis opened the document Mack had handed him and scanned the index page. Then he tossed it onto the desk. "I'll read that later while you two are…more pleasantly occupied." Travis smirked. "Let's just hit the highlights and lowlights. Have you discovered who our embezzler is?"

Since their father's illness, they'd discovered that someone on the staff had been stealing from the resort for several years. Uncovering the thief's identity was their top priority.

Mack frowned and folded his hands on the desk. "We're still working on that."

"But our forensic accountant discovered that most of the irregularities can be traced to food and beverage— the area where we need your help most," Grey added.

"So you expect me to revive the menu while working with a subpar chef who might also be the elusive embezzler neither of you nor your expensive forensic accountant could nail down? Well, that's just fucking great."

Travis walked over to the windows behind Mack that overlooked the property and provided a stunning view of the lake. He shoved his hands in his pockets.

Maybe if his brothers hadn't spent all their time pursuing romantic relationships, they would've found the thief by now.

"Let's begin with the obvious. We'll get rid of the mediocre chef and bring on someone with some real talent. Then if the current chef is the thief, we've solved both issues—the fast-food-grade menu and the embezzlement."

"We considered it," Grey acknowledged. "But Dad won't hear of it. You know how loyal he is. Hallie Gregson was Chef Fern's sous chef for years. When Fern up and left, Pops insisted on giving Hallie a shot as the executive chef. He believes she can become a world-class cook. Says she just needs a bit of—"

"Tutoring," Mack offered. "Which is what you do on those cooking shows, right?"

Mack had obviously *never* watched one of his shows.

"No, it isn't," Travis said impatiently. "I'm not a fairy godmother, Mack. I can't sprinkle pixie dust on this woman and make her a real chef. What I do is give self-taught chefs with *actual* talent the tools to achieve their destiny."

"Sounds like it came right out of the brochure." Grey chuckled.

Travis gave him the evil eye, then folded his arms. "Look, I want to help Pops and the resort, of course. But you're tying my hands and strapping a lead weight to my feet here."

"I thought you enjoyed a challenge."

Travis turned toward the sunny voice behind him and grinned.

"Molly. Good to see you." He hugged his sister-in-law. "And I do enjoy a good challenge, but I'm a chef and a mentor—*not* a miracle worker."

"*Yes*, you are," Molly countered confidently. "I've seen every episode of your shows. You've transformed self-taught chefs with raw talent and a complete lack of discipline into culinary superstars."

"That's kind of you to say, Mol." Travis realized that

his sister-in-law was stroking his ego, but it was nice to hear anyway.

The chefs he'd mentored were talented but had a lot to learn, as he once had. He'd had a natural gift in the kitchen and had been cooking since he was a kid, after his biological father died and his mother went off the rails. Then at fourteen, he'd decided he could do better than Jameson's suspect cooking. So he'd honed his skills under the tutelage of Moonlight Ridge's former executive chef, French ex-pat Henri Bernard.

Each week, Chef Henri had shown him how to prepare a new meal. Cooking relaxed him. And as he became more confident, he'd enjoyed adding his own flair and turning a basic meal into something spectacular.

Travis had derived immense satisfaction from watching his father and brothers devour the meals he'd made with such great care. But he'd never considered that being a chef was what he was meant to do with his life.

"I'm good," Travis said. "But I can't turn water into wine."

"I realize this may be your greatest challenge yet," Molly said, undeterred. "But our current staff, including the executive chef, are well aware things need to change if Moonlight Ridge is going to survive. They're all big fans and eager to work with you."

That bit of information made Travis feel the slightest bit hopeful. A self-aware chef who recognized the need for improvement was the kind of clay he could work with. Still…

"If you could turn things around here, it'd be quite the accomplishment," Molly added. "It'd make for a great book. And I'd bet one of those producer friends of yours would jump at the chance to document the process for a limited-run show. It'd mean more revenue for you and for Moonlight Ridge."

"Interesting idea, honey." Mack rubbed his chin. *Translation: he hated the idea.* "But should we really advertise that our current fare is…substandard?"

"We'd also need to invest in a serious upgrade of our kitchen and dining areas," Grey griped. "Moonlight Ridge can barely afford the renovations of the main building we're doing now. Let alone the cottages around the lake."

A mutually beneficial alliance that could make Moonlight Ridge better than ever *and* expand his restaurant brand, Traverser. That was a proposal worth considering.

Travis already had eateries in Atlanta—where he lived—and in LA—where they filmed the cooking network shows. Then there was the gastropub in London. His sights were set on opening signature restaurants in New York and perhaps Rome. Molly's idea could garner investors for his restaurant group and for Moonlight Ridge, which would ease the financial burden on the three of them.

"Brilliant idea, Molly," Travis said.

Molly looked pleased. Mack and Grey didn't.

"Didn't you hear anything I just said?" Mack asked.

"Sure. You said, *Bad publicity, wah, wah, wah.* Then Grey said, *We don't have the money, wah, wah, wah.*" Travis imitated the trombone-created voice of the adults talking in the Charlie Brown cartoons they'd watched as kids. "But to address your concern—by the time the show airs, the property will be fully renovated. As for the money, I'll run this by a couple of producer friends of mine. If they green-light the idea, I know I'll be able to raise the capital."

"You're talking about bringing in investors?" Mack stood, and Grey looked alarmed.

"Yeah, why?" Travis shrugged.

"You know how the old man feels about this place." Mack paced the floor. "If Pops isn't willing to make changes in staff, do you really think he'll relinquish control to investors?"

"He'd maintain a controlling interest in the place. The short-term investments would give us the money for renovations and the show would give us much-needed publicity. It's a win all the way around."

Travis sank onto his chair again and crossed one ankle over his knee.

"Good luck selling Pops on the idea." Grey chuckled.

"Now, that's a challenge I'll happily accept." Travis pointed at Grey, then sighed. "As for Hallie the Food Killer... I promise to do my best with her. If I succeed, I should be nominated for the culinary equivalent of knighthood."

Even Mack couldn't help laughing at that.

"I can't help you there," he said. "But you'll have Pops's undying gratitude and ours. Moonlight Ridge means everything to him, Travis. So I know you understand why saving this place means so much to all of us."

"Of course I do. The place means a lot to me, too." Travis's gaze drifted to the mahogany wood paneling and brass wall sconces original to the house. "I'll do everything I can to help save this place. I promise. In fact, I already have plans to meet with Chef Henri. Hopefully, he can help shorten the learning curve on some of the best local food suppliers and what diners in the area are looking for right now."

"Brilliant idea." Mack nodded.

Molly sat in on the remaining half hour of their meeting. The three of them brought him up to date on everything he needed to know to begin his monumental task of whipping the kitchen staff and catering operations into shape.

Autumn Kincaid knocked on the door as they were ending the meeting. She greeted Travis then asked if he'd be joining them for dinner.

"Wouldn't want to intrude on your double date. Besides, I need to head down to the kitchen and size up the staff. Then I'm spending the evening with Pops," Travis said.

"You wouldn't be intruding," Autumn assured him. "I made the reservation for the five of us. I assumed you'd be tagging along."

Tagging along? No thanks.

"Maybe some other time." Travis smiled.

Travis said his goodbyes, then watched as his brothers and their love interests walked toward the elevator hand in hand. He turned and headed back down the stairs.

Nope. Not even a little bit envious.

Sure, they all looked happy enough now. But relationships were constant work, and the payoff was usually disappointment, at best; betrayal, at worst.

Those weren't odds he was willing to play.

Unlike his lovestruck brothers, Travis would happily stick to his "bachelor life," get Moonlight Ridge's kitchen and catering services in shape, find the elusive embezzler then get back to his busy life in Atlanta and LA.

It was the least he could do for Jameson Holloway, who'd done so much for him.

Two

Riley George greeted the valet warmly as she exited her luxury SUV and handed the man her keys. It was nice being back in Asheville—the eclectic mountain town where she'd spent most of her summers when she was young.

During her two-hour drive from her home in Charlotte, Riley couldn't help reminiscing over those fun-filled summers at Moonlight Ridge and the boy who'd captured her heart.

But that had been a long time ago.

Riley was in Asheville on George Family Foundation business, not for a stroll down memory lane. So she would focus on the gala she was planning and all of the good it would do for an incredibly worthy charity. Not on the mistakes of her youth.

She stepped inside the enchanting little French restaurant owned and run by Chef Henri Bernard. Henri had been the executive chef at Moonlight Ridge when her family had stayed there. Ten years ago, he'd left to start a restaurant of his own. When the event committee had decided to have the gala in Asheville, Riley jumped at the opportunity to take the lead on it. Because she knew just the man to handle the catering: Chef Henri.

But Henri had called earlier in the week, insisting they needed to meet in person. So here she was with an uneasy feeling in her gut.

Riley followed the hostess through the charming restaurant that reminded her of the little bistros she frequented during her summers in Paris during college. The scent of savory sauces, fresh-baked bread and mouthwatering meats filled her nostrils.

Henri was seated in the private dining room with another man. The two of them were laughing. Chef Henri was still handsome. His salt-and-pepper goatee stood out against his warm brown skin. His shaved head was a good look for the gentle giant.

"It's lovely to see you." Henri's face lit up as he stood and gave her a *faire la bise*—the traditional French cheek kiss. "Thank you for agreeing to meet me here."

"Anything for you." She smiled at the older man who'd often spoiled her as a child with off-menu creations made just for her. "But I can wait until you're done with your meeting."

Riley glanced at his scowling companion, still seated. Her heart leaped into her throat. She'd recognize that face anywhere—even if it wasn't a regular fixture on cooking network shows. The features of his face had been branded into her memory.

"Travis?"

His dark eyes flamed, and she could practically feel the anger radiating off his dark brown skin. "Riley."

The detached tone of the man who'd been her first love sent a chill down her spine. Instantly, she'd reverted from a confident, professional woman to the teenage girl who was torn between the boy she was head over heels for and her disapproving parents.

You're not that girl anymore. Don't let anyone make you feel that way. Not even Travis.

Riley stood taller and offered Henri a warm smile that hopefully conveyed more confidence than she felt. "I'm early. I'll grab a bite at the bar while you two finish up."

She was in no hurry; she'd booked a hotel for the night.

"No need, I was just leaving." Travis pushed his chair back.

"No one is going anywhere." Chef Henri glanced between them sternly. "I invited you both here for a very important reason. All I ask is that you hear me out."

The beloved chef knew full well neither of them would deny his request.

Travis nodded, then hailed the server. He ordered a boulevardier made with King's Finest bourbon. Apparently, a conversation with her required a cocktail.

But how could she blame him after what she'd done?

Riley sat down and folded her hands on the table. She turned her attention toward Chef Henri. "Okay, Henri. What is this about?"

"It's about the gala." There was a pained look on Henri's face.

Riley's pulse quickened. "Is there a problem with the menu?"

"It's much bigger than that," Henri said. "I've been

given the opportunity to open a restaurant in Paris. Something I have always dreamed of."

"That's wonderful news, Henri. Congratulations!" Riley squeezed his forearm.

Travis seemed pleased, but not surprised. He apparently already knew.

"Unfortunately, I would be required to go to Paris very soon, and I would be there indefinitely."

Panic tightened Riley's chest. "But that means…"

"That is correct. I cannot accept this opportunity *and* headline your gala."

Riley's head spun with a million little details. Like the stack of postcards she'd had printed with Chef Henri's face on them and the menu they'd created together so painstakingly.

"This event is built on the draw of a high-profile chef who'll mingle with the guests," Henri continued. "So if this will cause irreparable harm to your organization, I will pass on the opportunity."

"No. I'll figure something out." Riley was momentarily shaken from her thoughts about the countless phone calls she'd need to make. They'd need to postpone the event or perhaps cancel it altogether. "I'd never ask you to give up the chance to fulfill a lifelong dream, Henri."

"I appreciate that, Riley." Chef Henri gave her a grateful smile. "But I have a solution that could work out for all three of us."

"Wait…what?" Travis looked up from his phone.

Henri ignored his former protégé's question. His gaze remained firmly on hers. "Travis will be here in Asheville for the next few months."

Travis set his drink on the table with a thud and sat ramrod straight, his back pressed against the wall.

"You're volunteering me for this…this charity thing of hers?"

"I'm not *volunteering* you," Henri corrected him, his voice stern. "It is obviously up to you whether you will accept the project. However, the serendipity of you calling to ask for advice on raising Moonlight Ridge's profile when I was just about to tell Riley I could not do her event… Well, that I couldn't ignore. Especially given how close you two once were."

Riley and Travis had hidden their relationship from their parents as teens. But Henri and Travis's brothers had been aware of it. And they'd kept their secret.

"That was a long time ago, Chef H, and you know how things ended," Travis said.

"I do. And it's time you two found a way to let go of what happened that night." Henri's voice was heavy with sadness. "More importantly, you are both smart, professional businesspeople. Therefore, you must see how ideal this collaboration is. Travis is a *true* celebrity chef. Your guests will be thrilled by the upgrade. In fact, I believe you will need a *bigger* venue." Henri looked at Travis pointedly.

Travis's eyes widened, as if he understood but didn't like whatever message Henri was silently conveying. He didn't meet her gaze. Instead, he spoke directly to Henri.

"The mighty George family has never been fond of me. I doubt they'd want me headlining their event," Travis scoffed.

"Then this is your chance to prove them wrong," Henri said before turning back toward her. "Would your parents object?"

"I run the foundation, so my parents won't be a problem," Riley said firmly. "But even if Travis was amenable to headlining the event, finding a larger venue isn't an option at this late date. Besides, we're locked in a contract with the current venue."

"And between my plans for the next Traverser restaurant, my obligations with the cooking network and helping to manage Moonlight Ridge, my hands are full, Henri. While I'm here, my priorities are making sure Pops is on the mend and that Moonlight Ridge—"

"Jameson isn't well?" Riley had always been fond of Travis's father, the owner of Moonlight Ridge.

Travis gave her his full attention for the first time since she'd arrived. "My father had a serious brain health issue a few months ago. He's much better now, but seeing after Pops and getting Moonlight Ridge back on track are my current priorities."

"*That* is why I am referring this event to you." Henri tapped the table with one of his thick fingers. "It is a high-profile event that will garner press statewide. Is that not so, Riley?"

"Right. Yes." She took Henri's cue. "There will be lots of press coverage leading up to the event."

"And with you headlining, there will be national interest," Henri continued. "What better way to showcase Moonlight Ridge's new menu and the venue itself...if the event is moved?"

Travis rubbed his stubbled chin thoughtfully, and Riley's belly tightened.

The sensory memory of running her palm along his chin and teasing him about his stubble tugged at something in her chest. It cracked the lid on the storehouse of memories she kept locked away there. Sweet moments with her first love whom she could never quite forget. No matter how hard she tried.

The flashback of that fond memory made her smile. But then she recalled the pain and anger in Travis's eyes the last time she'd seen him. He'd looked at her as if she'd stabbed him in the heart and turned the knife. As if she was the cruelest person on the face of the earth.

And maybe she had been.

"Are we talking about changing the menu?" Riley's mind finally caught up to their conversation. Both men stared at her as if it should be obvious that a change in chef would require a change in menu.

"The recipes I create are proprietary, of course, *ma chérie.*" Henri placed a gentle hand on her forearm. "I thought you knew."

She did; she just hadn't expected it to be an issue.

Deep breaths. Working with Travis on one project isn't the end of the world.

More important, she needed his help. *Desperately.*

Given the flare of Travis's nostrils and the arch of his thick brow, he was well aware of this. *If* Travis agreed to help her, it wouldn't be in the spirit of letting bygones be bygones. He was going to make this as difficult as possible.

Riley swallowed her well-honed George pride and her own distaste for needing anything from anyone.

Despite her family's wealth and her healthy bank account, she was beholden to her family in many ways. She was thirty-two years old and the bulk of the money left to her by her obscenely wealthy grandfather came with two conditions. She had to reach the age of thirty *and* be married to a "man of independent means"—a requirement not made of her male counterparts.

Her grandfather and parents were displeased that she'd secretly dated Travis as a teen. Nor did they appreciate her gravitation toward men whose families were of modest means. Most of them had been perfectly wonderful human beings—as Travis had been. But two notable exceptions—one in college and one in grad school—had turned out to be as interested in her family's fortune as her family had predicted.

Her grandfather had lectured her about having too big a heart, which she wore on her sleeve. He'd worried she'd end up with some "worthless cad" who'd drain her bank account. So he'd added the marriage stipulation before she could receive full control of her trust.

Needing something from anyone—especially from a man—set her teeth on edge. But Travis obviously wanted to see her beg. So, for the sake of the charity and the hundreds of people it would benefit, just this once she would.

"Travis, I realize this would be quite an imposition, but this event is important. So if you could step in for Chef Henri, I can't tell you how grateful I'd be."

"Actually, that's *exactly* what I'd like to hear." Travis smirked.

Riley's belly fluttered as his eyes swept over her.

Is Travis implying that—

"Monetarily." Travis rubbed a thumb and two fingers together.

"Oh, yes, of course. Money." Riley's cheeks burned with embarrassment.

How could she have thought, even for a moment, that Travis had been referring to something more…*personal*?

Riley pulled a pad and pen from her handbag. She jotted down the same generous figure she and Henri had agreed to. Then she slid it across the table.

Travis glanced at the number, then slid it back.

"Try again, RG. That isn't enough to make me get

out of bed, let alone take on a last-minute project that I'd be revamping from scratch." He shifted his gaze to his mentor, who chuckled and shook his head. "No offense, Chef H."

"None taken, son. I taught you to know your worth and charge accordingly," Henri said. "But keep in mind that Riley is an old friend, and you would be doing this as a favor to me." He turned to her and smiled. "I must prepare your meal. Your usual?"

"Please." The tension in her shoulders eased. Riley loved that Henri took great delight in preparing his delicious coq au champagne for her himself.

"I will leave you two to work out the details. Thank you for being so understanding, *ma chérie*."

Travis drained the last of his boulevardier. "Okay, let's talk money."

Riley ordered a drink of her own, rattled not by the impending negotiations but by the man seated on the opposite side of the table who thought her a cruel, unfeeling monster. She hated that, after all these years, what Travis Holloway thought of her still mattered.

Three

"You want *twice* what we were going to pay Chef Henri?" Riley's eyes widened.

She kept her tone neutral, but her aggravation was evident in the stiffening of her narrow shoulders and the way her warm brown skin glowed red across her nose and cheeks. The same cheeks he'd once peppered with soft, slow kisses before he'd eventually kissed her full lips.

Travis fought off the visceral memory of Riley's heavenly scent and the warmth of her skin as he'd held her in his arms one summer evening when they'd met in the woods near the pond at the rear of the property. His back had been pressed against the rough bark of a red maple tree as she'd stared up at him and told him she loved him.

He'd wanted to believe that a girl as sweet and beautiful as Riley George had a thing for him. And he'd fallen hard, fast and deep. But it had all been an act. A rich kid slumming it with the help for a couple of summers. Until it had stopped being fun for her. Then she'd been ready to move on to a guy whose family had even more money than hers.

When she'd ended it abruptly, Travis had been gutted. He'd reacted badly.

"This is a charity gala, Travis." Riley's strictly business demeanor shook him from his daze.

"That's why I'm not charging my usual appearance fee."

"Right." Riley crumpled the piece of paper and raised her eyes to his. "Still, it's a considerable increase in our planned expenses."

"True, but if you go with a larger venue, you can capitalize on a considerable bump in ticket sales." He wasn't being cocky; just stating the obvious.

"I'd love to go bigger to take advantage of your *celebrity chef* status." Riley uttered the term as if it was distasteful. "But we're locked in a contract with our current venue."

"Where and when is the event booked?" When she told him, Travis nodded. "Popular wedding venue. They keep a list of couples on standby, so they can easily rebook the space, if needed."

Chef Henri had set him up with the alley-oop. Now it was time for the slam dunk.

"Alice, the coordinator there, owes my father a favor. I can get her to release you from the contract with a minimal cancellation fee."

"Even if that's true, it would be impossible to find another venue at this late date. My event is in seven weeks," Riley said.

"I just checked." Travis gestured to his phone. "Our

grand ballroom is available on that date, so we can accommodate about twice as many guests as your current venue. I'll do whatever I can to help sell out the event and bring in additional sponsorships. You'll make back my additional fee and double your revenue."

"You're suggesting we move the event to Moonlight Ridge?" Her tone was incredulous. "I mean… I know the place was glamorous in its heyday, but I've heard… I mean… I'm not sure it's right for the kind of event I'm trying to put on here."

Travis tried to relax the scowl that slid into place the moment he'd recognized Riley. His heart had thundered in his chest as he recalled the events that unfolded the night of the accident.

When he'd first shown an interest in Riley, Mack had warned him it wouldn't end well. His brother had been right. But Travis had never imagined it would cost his family…everything. It seemed only right that Riley would help them reclaim some of what they'd lost.

"I understand your reservations," Travis said calmly. "And that might've been true a few months ago. But Mack and Grey have made vast improvements to the place in the past several months. And I'm here now to continue those efforts."

"The three of you are working on this…*together*?"

Travis narrowed his gaze at her, then thanked the server who'd brought him another boulevardier, courtesy of Chef Henri.

Riley and Chef H had been discussing more than just gala themes and dinner menus. How else would she know things had been tense between him and his brothers? Was she keeping tabs on them?

He certainly hadn't been following her. In fact, he'd tried to scrub Riley George from his brain.

Clearly, he hadn't been successful.

"I have fond memories of Moonlight Ridge, and I'm thrilled that you and your brothers are restoring it. But—"

"Moving the event to Moonlight Ridge is a nonnegotiable part of this deal." Travis had the leverage here, and he was going to use it.

"You're hijacking my event by making a change of venue a *requirement*?" Riley's expression went from apologetic to indignant, her nostrils flaring. "That isn't fair."

"*Hijacking?* That's a bit dramatic." Travis calmly sipped his drink, enjoying Riley's sense of outrage a little more than he should.

"You're blackmailing me into moving my event to your…your…run-down shack of a hotel." Riley folded her arms.

Gloves off, huh? Okay, let's go.

"First, 'run-down shack of a hotel' is harsh and categorically untrue, in light of all the renovations we've already completed, *Princess*." Travis used the term of endearment often employed by Riley's father. Something he'd teased her with when they were kids. "Second, blackmail implies coercion. I'm not *coercing* you into this deal. Hell, I don't even want to do this. But if you want me for your little charity shindig, you'll have to pay to play. And this, RG, is the price of admission. Double the booking fee, which you'll easily recoup, and make Moonlight Ridge your new, *larger* venue." He ticked each item off on his fingers. "Take it or leave it. I don't really care either way. Personally, I'm hoping you pass on the deal."

There was a momentary crack in her cool demeanor.

A flash of what seemed like genuine hurt. Not that *genuine* was a word he'd associate with any member of the George family.

Travis glanced at his watch, then stood and dropped a tip on the table for the server.

"Let me know what you decide, but keep in mind that with the new renovations and Mack's new brewery opening on-site, that date will book out soon." He made his way toward the exit to the parking lot.

"Travis... Wait!"

He halted in response to Riley's voice, strung tight with frustration. When he turned around, she was standing in front of him.

His eyes trailed down, involuntarily, to her legs, which looked a mile long in tall designer heels. Her silk blouse revealed a hint of cleavage between her full breasts. A slim skirt skimmed her curvy hips and a small slit rose a few inches above her knee, revealing the smooth brown skin of her lean thighs. All of which made his heart beat faster. Heat rose up his neck.

Riley folded her arms and glared at him.

Had she caught him checking her out? Or was she just pissed because someone other than a George was calling the shots? The latter gave him great pleasure. Giving her the impression he was still attracted to her did not. Especially since it was true.

Riley looked *incredible*.

"I'll need to see the event space before I decide." Her quiet control had returned.

He was just another vendor to her; not the boy she'd once claimed to love. The boy she'd sneaked out to meet by the pond. Who'd taught her to fish and skip stones across the water.

So he shouldn't let their past cloud his judgment, either.

"You can tour the place anytime you like." Travis handed her a business card. "Just call to make an appointment."

"This is the number to the front desk?" Riley seemed insulted.

"Ask for Molly Haskell-Holloway. She manages the resort. She'll show you the ballroom space, answer your questions and book the date, if you choose."

"Mack's girlfriend, Molly?"

"Mack's *wife*, Molly," Travis corrected.

"I'd need to work closely with the chef…with you…on this, especially since we're revamping the menu." Riley tucked her hair behind her ear. "I'm sure Mack's wife is a very nice person, but I'm making this deal with you, Travis. Not the hotel or your family."

Travis groaned, then pulled a different card from his wallet. He handed it to her. "That's my private business line. Call me when you're ready. I'll schedule a tour with me *and* Molly."

Riley accepted the card. "If the tour goes well, I'll also need to spend a night or two at the resort before I can recommend Moonlight Ridge for lodging."

"If you decide to move forward, Molly will see to it." Travis glanced at his watch again. He was trying to instill the need for order and discipline in the kitchen staff. Arriving late to his own meeting wouldn't be a good look. "I really have to go."

Travis left without waiting for a response. Because there was no one on the planet he was less interested in than Riley George.

He didn't blame her for the accident anymore. Still, he'd allowed his obsession with the hedge-fund princess to fuck up his life once. He wouldn't do it again.

Four

Riley pulled up to the familiar stone fence and wrought iron gate with its welcoming Moonlight Ridge sign in black script. She hadn't seen this beautiful, historic property in fifteen years. Yet, despite fond memories of the place, she was filled with a sense of dread.

The horrible mistake she'd made one summer night had poisoned those memories and ruined so many lives and relationships.

It was good to hear Travis and his brothers were working together on restoring Moonlight Ridge. Learning of its decline had broken her heart. But she'd been gutted to learn what had happened to Travis and that the tragedy had caused a rift between the brothers. According to Henri, they'd grown apart, each brother blaming himself for the accident and burdened by the guilt. Each of them struggling with the fallout of that horrible night.

Like Travis, Mack and Grey, she, too, blamed herself. But rehashing the past was useless. It wouldn't turn back time or change what had happened.

For months afterward, Riley had been plagued by nightmares, the events of that night replaying in her brain. Each time it ended exactly the same. With Mack's truck in a tangled, bloody mess.

Riley inhaled deeply and tried to forget the ugly past as she followed the winding drive that led to the main building. Moonlight Ridge was a fine estate, if a little dated and worse for wear. And despite her objections to Travis strong-arming her into moving the event here, Moonlight Ridge had the potential to be a far better venue for her *Great Gatsby*–themed gala.

The event would raise money for one of her favorite charities. One of the many causes her family's foundation helped each year.

Once she'd handed her keys to the valet and followed the bellman inside, Riley glanced around at the old place. There was something so magical about the ornate desk with all its decorative details that were a throwback to the 1930s, when the home was built.

She could still remember Travis telling her the story of how the original owners had acquired the front desk from an abandoned hotel built in the same period. It'd been transported there in the 1950s, when they'd turned their family estate into a resort for their wealthy friends.

Riley had always been fascinated by the history and architecture of this old place with its original lighting fixtures; stunning, regal staircase; and countless other historic architectural details that made the art and history geek in her giddy with joy.

She'd liked that the building was lovingly worn, like a

favorite pair of old shoes. But to Travis's credit, there had been many updates to the lobby and exterior that brought back some of Moonlight Ridge's old Hollywood charm.

But would it be enough to compete with the growing number of luxury hotels in the area?

"Ms. George." A beautiful young woman with messy blond curls and mesmerizing eyes somewhere between gray and green approached with her hand extended. "Welcome back to Moonlight Ridge. I'm the manager, Molly Haskell-Holloway."

"It's good to see you again, Molly." Riley shook the woman's hand warmly.

"I didn't think you'd remember me." Molly's smile broadened, then she asked the bellman to take Riley's bags to her room.

"You remember me." Riley followed the woman as she walked in the direction of the ballrooms. "Why wouldn't I remember you?"

Molly tucked a few of her wayward blond curls behind her ear. "Because I was an insecure kid whose dad was the help, and you were the glamorous Riley George."

They stopped in front of the double doors that led to the ballroom.

"I know it seemed like I led a perfect, charmed life," Riley said. "But things aren't always as rosy as they seem from the outside."

The other woman's mouth fell open and she seemed to be at a loss for words.

Riley hadn't meant to make things uncomfortable; she was just being honest. Yes, she was from an ultra-wealthy family, but they were emotionally distant, leaving her feeling isolated. She'd often wished her family was as close as Jameson and his sons were.

"I look forward to seeing the ballroom again," Riley said, eager to alleviate the sudden awkwardness.

"I've always loved this old ballroom, but wait until you see it now." Molly beamed.

Riley glanced around. "Will Travis be joining us?"

Molly tried to hide a knowing smile. "He'll join us later. Promise."

Riley's cheeks heated. *Great.* Now Travis's sister-in-law would think she still had a thing for him. Which she absolutely did not. Despite how enticing he'd looked in that pair of dark-wash jeans and a button-down dress shirt that fit snugly over his biceps and broad shoulders.

Not that she'd noticed.

"I just need to talk to him about the theme and menu," Riley said nonchalantly.

"Of course. Right this way." Molly opened the doors and turned on the lights.

"It's beautiful." Riley stared around the room, her eyes a little misty. She'd attended her first formal dance there as a tween.

"It is, isn't it?" Molly seemed as mesmerized by the enchanting space as Riley. "It's always been one of my favorite places in the building."

"Mine, too." Riley walked through the space set up with round tables covered in white tablecloths. "It looks smaller than it did when I was a kid."

Molly noted the temporary walls that had been installed to divide the room up into three separate spaces that could be rented out simultaneously.

"We're having a luncheon here tomorrow and only needed this center space. But for your event, we'll use the room at full capacity." Molly grinned. "So, if you're ready for your tour, I'll take you through the space, we'll look at a few of the cottages on the property then we'll come back here and meet with Travis."

"Sounds perfect." Riley tried to ignore the fluttering in her belly whenever Molly mentioned Travis's name.

Travis followed the sound of Molly's and Riley's voices to the conference room. He gritted his teeth and tried to tamp down his conflicting feelings for his ex. Feelings he'd tried to erase long ago.

He'd lived in a world where Riley George no longer existed, and it had suited him just fine. So if he hadn't been seated when Riley walked into that restaurant, seeing her again would've knocked him on his ass.

She was still stunningly gorgeous. In fact, she'd gotten more beautiful. And while she'd always had an enticing figure, her fuller curves were tantalizing.

Don't even think about it.

Travis shook his head, trying to jostle the vision of Riley in that little skirt from his brain.

Riley George was a potential client who could help accelerate their plans to rebrand Moonlight Ridge and make it relevant again. She was a means to an end, as he'd obviously been for her.

Travis stepped through the open door and Riley's gaze immediately met his. An unsettling warmth spread through his chest.

"Thanks for meeting with me, Travis. I realize you have a lot on your plate right now."

"I do, but Moonlight Ridge is a top priority. So I'll do everything in my power to ensure this event exceeds your expectations." He accepted a document from Molly that laid out the specifics of the event.

He froze when he saw the name of the charity.

"You said this was one of your favorite charities."
Travis glanced up at her.

"It is. They do important work and the organization
is well run."

The organization helped teenagers who'd aged out of
the foster system transition to life as independent adults.
It was a charity he often supported, too.

Travis was aware of how lucky he and his brothers
had been. Countless older kids in the system never found
families. And transitioning to adulthood without a support system wasn't easy, so the work this organization
did was vitally important.

"How long have you been working with this charity?"
It wasn't relevant to this meeting or his ability to plan the
menu. Yet, he needed to know.

"I began volunteering for them as an undergrad. When
I started working for our family's foundation, I insisted
we make it one of our top-tier organizations," Riley said.

What kind of head game is she playing?

She'd known that he'd come to Jameson as a foster
child. Was that why she'd chosen this nonprofit?

"It's an organization that's important to all of us here,
too." Molly placed a gentle hand on Travis's arm, bringing him out of his temporary daze. "So rest assured that
we'll all work hard to ensure that this event is spectacular
and goes off without a hitch."

Travis gave his sister-in-law a discreet nod of gratitude for getting him back on track.

So Riley and the George Family Foundation had a
charitable streak. That didn't mean they were nice people. And it certainly didn't mean he should let down his
guard.

Five

Riley settled into her room, obviously one that had been recently renovated. The classic architecture was still there, but the bathroom was updated, the bedding, window treatments and carpeting were new and there was a large-screen television in the room.

The resort was a gorgeous space that fit with her *Great Gatsby* theme. Her parents wouldn't be happy about her moving the event to Moonlight Ridge, but when it came to the foundation, she had the final say. She was at least thankful to her grandfather for that.

Riley's phone buzzed. She checked the caller ID and sucked in a deep breath. She'd hired a team of expensive lawyers to contest her grandfather's will, and she'd been eagerly waiting to hear from them.

"Devon, tell me you have good news." Riley didn't bother with small talk. She was paying this man an obscene hourly fee. What she wanted was results. Pure and simple.

The older man drew in a long breath, and a stone formed in the pit of Riley's stomach.

"I'm sorry, Miss George. I wish I had better news. But your grandfather made his will ironclad. He was of sound mind at the time, so we have no grounds on which to contest it. And believe me, we've tried to come at this from every possible angle."

Riley's pulse throbbed and her head ached.

"This is a bunch of sexist bullshit," she muttered, more to herself than him.

"I couldn't agree more, Miss George," the man said. "But the bottom line is that it was your grandfather's money to distribute as he saw fit. Now, there is some room to interpret exactly what 'a man of independent means' entails, but unfortunately there's no way around the marriage requirement."

"So your best advice is there's nothing I can do?" She sank onto the bed.

"Officially? I'm afraid so."

"But *unofficially*?" she prompted.

"Unofficially, if it were me, I'd make an *arrangement* with a man of means. Draw up an airtight agreement of your own and get married for one year. He gets something out of the deal, and you get full access to your sizable trust. It's a win for both of you."

"A marriage of convenience? *That's* your best advice, Devon? I'm not living in a regency romance novel. Why should I have to jump through hoops to get *my* money?" she demanded.

"Because until you fulfill the requirements of your grandfather's will, it's still very much *his* money," Devon

Myers reminded her. "I'm sorry, Miss George. I wish I had better news for you."

"So do I." Riley ended the call and stifled the scream building at the back of her throat.

"Make an arrangement with a man of means," Riley muttered as she paced the floor angrily, her heart racing. "Is he kidding?"

Devon better not bill me for that stupid-ass advice.

She wasn't involved with anyone right now, and because of her busy work life, she hadn't been for some time. So where was she supposed to get this wealthy fake husband?

Even if she was involved with someone, a deal like this would be the kiss of death for the relationship. Her money—or their lack of it—had been at the root of the disintegration of every romantic relationship that had ever really meant anything to her.

There was the longtime boyfriend turned fiancé who'd ended their engagement when she'd refused to cosign a terrible land deal for him. College boyfriends more interested in her last name and family's bank account than her. The guy she adored who was uncomfortable around her family and friends. And Travis—her first love whom she'd ended it with because her family hadn't approved of him.

She obviously wasn't winning at this whole relationship thing, despite how perfect and glamorous Molly Haskell-Holloway believed her life to be.

Riley stared out of the window at the extensive property. The Moonlight Ridge estate was still picturesque and serene with all of its lush green trees that would soon be turning lovely shades of orange, yellow and red.

As a teen, Riley had found solace in hiking the beautiful trail around the lake. Sometimes she'd ventured deeper into the property to a lovely little bench beside the small pond in the woods where she and Travis would eventually begin to meet. Their initials were carved underneath the bench.

There's nothing fresh air and a little exercise can't fix.

It was her grandmother's philosophy, and exactly what she needed right now.

She'd change out of her business clothes and take a brisk walk in the woods. Maybe the fresh air and exercise would rev up her brain cells. Then she'd fire Devon and that bunch of useless lawyers and find another law firm that would be more diligent about getting her out from under the archaic parameters of her grandfather's will.

Travis changed into his running shorts, shirt and shoes. He honestly hated jogging. But after the two years of recovery required for him to be able to run again, he'd learned not to take it for granted. Besides, it always helped clear his head, which was exactly what he needed. Because Riley George had commandeered premium space in his brain.

He was physically tired after a long day, but mentally exhausted. He'd spent the past two days working with the executive chef, Hallie Gregson; the events and catering manager, Ross Barnes; and the kitchen and catering staff.

As promised, Hallie was eager to learn new techniques. She'd nailed every single task he'd given her. She understood that this was about saving Moonlight Ridge. Ross, on the other hand, was less open to change.

Travis got it. Nobody liked the implication that they were shit at their job. And grown men who thought they knew it all were particularly resistant to guidance. But he'd dealt with plenty of overblown egos. He could handle a guy whose pride was hurt.

Ross would just have to get over himself.

After stretching, Travis stepped outside into the crisp mountain air. He was staying in the same cottage where he and Riley had sometimes met. Being at the very back of the property, it was the least desirable, and often the last to be booked. It seemed ironic when Harry at the front desk had assigned him to this cottage. But now that Riley had waltzed back into his life, it felt like a cruel cosmic joke.

The universe was fucking with him, and maybe he deserved it.

Travis secured the door and took the path that went toward the lake. Riley George's words still rang in his head.

So you're blackmailing me into moving my event to your run-down shack of a hotel.

Maybe he had. And he wasn't sorry about it, either. The George family—including Princess Riley—had been a collective ass to him. He was doing this event as a favor to Henri, but also because he'd do whatever it took to help make Moonlight Ridge successful again. If he got the chance to relish the sweet taste of a little payback while helping out the people he cared about, all the better.

Travis picked up the pace of his run, his heart pumping harder as he tried to outrun the vision of Riley George in that cleavage-bearing top and hip-hugging skirt. But he couldn't; the image was tattooed on his brain.

Travis followed the trail, pushing himself harder than he had in a long time. Hoping the exertion would take his mind off Riley George. Finally, he came to a little clearing by the lake where he'd often gone to sit and think while he was growing up here on the estate. His gaze swept the property.

Much of the main building had been renovated, and they'd made several landscaping upgrades. However, several of the outbuildings were in need of repair and a fresh coat of paint, including the old building on the lake that was once a little café. It'd been closed since Chef Henri's departure. Mack's brewery would be opening on the property in a few weeks. If it and their efforts with the resort were successful, maybe he could convert the old café into a signature Traverser restaurant. It was something he'd dreamed about since he'd first become a chef.

"Chef Henri made the best Belgian waffles there for Sunday brunch."

Travis turned quickly toward the voice behind him.

Riley Frickin' George.

Because of course it was. Evidently, seeing her twice in one day hadn't been enough.

Be nice. Right now, she's not your ex; she's a Moonlight Ridge client.

Travis silently assessed the hot-pink tank top and black leggings that highlighted Riley's finer assets. God, she looked amazing. Not that it mattered. Because he wasn't interested.

Been there. Done that. Got the scars, the shattered dreams and a metal screw in my leg to show for it.

"You aren't stalking me are you, RG?" He was only half joking.

"Don't flatter yourself, Holloway." Riley plunked down on a large rock. "I needed some fresh air, and I just kind of ended up here."

"Same." Travis picked up a pebble and skipped it across the lake.

Riley's soft laugh pulled his attention to her. Her beauty was stunning, and her soft smile and warm laughter had always filled him with contentment. But that was then.

"Think you can do better?" he asked with an involuntary grin.

"I know I can." She hopped off the rock and dusted off her bottom, drawing his attention there.

His cock tightened in his shorts.

Riley stood beside him on the shore; her floral scent—honeysuckle maybe—tickled his nostrils. She stooped down to pick up a handful of stones, then opened her palm.

"Three for you. Three for me. Best two out of three wins," she said confidently.

Travis lifted a brow as he studied her. He picked three stones from her palm, careful his skin didn't touch hers. "You sure you want to go up against the master, Princess?"

Riley rolled her eyes. "If you're scared, maybe you should call your big brothers."

"Oh! And she's talking shit, too. Yeah, I'm definitely down for this." Travis weighed the stone in his hand. "Ladies first. But try not to take this ass-whipping I'm about to hand you personally."

"Duly noted." Riley stepped forward, positioned her body sideways—in a way that gave him a perfect view of her mouthwatering profile. Then she pitched her arm forward as the stone went skipping across the water.

"Not bad, Princess. We've got ourselves a ringer here. You've been practicing."

She lifted her bare shoulders. "Maybe you should've asked me that before our little bet."

"Oh, now it's a bet?" Travis turned to her. "And what exactly does the winner get?"

Riley frowned, her mouth twisting. "I haven't thought that far. How about we make it a favor to be named at a later date?"

"Sounds open-ended as hell and hella dangerous." Travis studied her for a moment before turning toward the water. "But you're on."

He pitched the stone, skipping it across the water. It went a few feet beyond where hers had sunk into the lake. "Point for me."

Riley bounced on her heels, shook out her shoulders and rolled her neck, her ponytail waving behind her. She looked like a prizefighter preparing to enter the ring.

Travis couldn't help chuckling. He honestly didn't want to be amused by Riley George. But she was cute as hell with her competitive self.

Obviously, that hadn't changed. Challenging him to a run was how she'd first gotten his attention when they were teens.

She'd beaten him handily.

Riley pitched her next stone. It skipped on the water three times before sinking.

Nice, but not unbeatable.

He stepped up and pitched his next stone. It skipped three times, too. But it sank just short of the ripple where hers had.

Shit.

"Point for me!" Riley squealed, gleefully. "So this one is for the win."

Riley pitched the next stone and it skipped four times before eventually sinking into the water some distance away.

Impressive. But still not unbeatable. He'd done better.

Travis rolled his right shoulder, which still ached

sometimes from the crash. But it locked up as he pitched his arm forward, and the stone plunked and sank to the bottom rather than skipping across the water.

Don't be a sore loser. It's a stupid stone-skipping contest.

Travis turned to Riley, who was pumping her arm in the air and doing a little dance that made his dick twitch.

"Congrats, Princess. You won." He wiped his hands together to remove the sand. "Good for you. I'd hold on to that favor for when we start working on your event menu."

"I'll keep that in mind." Riley rubbed her hands on her thighs. "Speaking of which, do you think you'll have some time tomorrow to work on the menu?"

"I'm booked. Got meetings with the staff here and with the network production team."

"But I'm only booked for one night. I was hoping we could take care of this while I'm here."

"Look, I realize you're accustomed to people dropping everything and rearranging their schedules for you," Travis said calmly. "But I was pretty clear about how packed my schedule is. So if you need someone who's more readily available, I understand."

"No, I'll just stay another night." Riley stared out onto the water.

"Great. We can meet over breakfast on Friday morning. I'm free then."

"Perfect." Riley offered a weak smile.

"It's getting late. I'm headed to my dad's house, but I can walk you back to the resort." He hoped she'd pass on his offer.

"I'd appreciate that." Riley started back toward the trail and he walked beside her in silence. "By the way, congratulations on your success with Traverser and your cooking network shows. You've done some amazing things, Travis."

"Thanks." Her seemingly sincere compliment was unexpected.

"When did you know you wanted to be a chef?"

Travis halted, narrowing his gaze at her. Was she deliberately being obtuse? When did she think he *decided* that this was what he wanted to do with his life?

"Oh, I... I should've thought... I'm sorry." Riley's sweet expression crumpled. She seemed genuinely horrified by her misstep. "Of course, I know the accident changed your career prospects. But you've always loved to cook. I just wondered...never mind." She turned to walk again.

Travis fell into step beside her. The silence between them felt like a thick, choking cloud of smoke. Finally, he answered her. Mostly because he couldn't stand the weird silence.

"I spent the better part of a year in a wheelchair," he said. "So it became obvious that I'd need to find another line of work. Cooking was something I was good at and enjoyed, so Chef H encouraged me to pursue it as a career. Besides, it was a way to burn off my anger."

"I didn't know," Riley said softly. She stopped and turned toward him with a pained expression. "I knew your injuries were serious, but I didn't realize you'd been confined to..." The indomitable Riley George looked flustered. She tucked loose strands of hair behind her ear. "I'm sorry, Travis," she blurted suddenly, her big brown eyes going wide. "I've wanted to tell you that since that night, but I never got the chance. It's been eating away at me all this time."

His shoulders stiffened, but he didn't respond. He didn't need the princess's apology, and he sure as hell didn't want her pity. Not then. Not now.

He'd done just fine without either.

Travis continued toward the resort, and Riley fell into step, despite his faster pace.

"I understand why you didn't want to see me at the hospital and why you wouldn't take my calls," she said, slightly winded. "But I'm sorry about everything and… Travis, wait. *Please.*"

Riley grabbed his forearm, forcing him to stop. He dropped his unsmiling gaze to where her skin touched his. She immediately withdrew her hand.

"I know you're still angry with me and that maybe you'll never be able to forgive me for that night. I don't blame you. But I still needed to say I'm sorry for my role in what happened."

Travis wasn't interested in revisiting the past. He didn't blame Riley or anyone for what happened. It was just an accident. But she'd been awful to him that night, and he wasn't here to absolve her of any guilt she might still feel over it. That was her problem.

"The main building is just up ahead." He pointed. "You'll be fine from here, right?"

She nodded, the corners of her eyes wet. "Yes, thank you. I'll see you on Friday."

He grunted in acknowledgment, then jogged toward his dad's, running as fast as he could, his legs and lungs burning. Determined to get all thoughts of Riley George out of his head.

Six

Riley stood in front of the mirror in her room, fretting over the skirt and blouse she'd chosen. This was a business meeting, not a date. Yet, she'd changed twice this morning and had put in a little extra effort with her makeup. Because even though Travis Holloway clearly didn't want to spend a second more with her than necessary, she couldn't help wanting him to forgive her. Or at the least not to hate her.

Running into him at the lake had been unexpected, but it had been nice to do something as benign together as skipping stones on the lake. There was even a moment when he'd actually smiled at her. Albeit begrudgingly. But then she'd needed to absolve herself of some of the guilt she felt by apologizing to him.

Clearly, he hadn't wanted her apology. Rather than clearing the air between them, her words seemed to dig up all of the pain and the anger simmering below Travis's cool facade.

Riley raked her fingers through her tousled waves, grabbed her purse and portfolio and headed for the third floor, where the offices were located. When she got off the elevator, the smell of bacon led her to the small conference room where she was meeting Travis.

"This smells amazing." Riley's stomach rumbled in response to the delicious smell. After a walk on the trail that morning, she was starving.

Travis stood, his gaze trailing down her body appreciatively for a moment. But then he frowned and returned to his seat. His eyes were glued to the electronic pad on the table in front of him. "Grab a plate, then we'll get started. Hopefully, we can knock this out in—" he glanced at his all-black Shinola chronograph watch "—an hour tops."

Riley set her things on the table and grabbed a plate, her skin tingling from his brief but heated gaze.

Travis typed out the last of his notes from their meeting. They'd quickly agreed on a new menu, based on the old one. Next, he'd conduct a tasting for her final approval the following week. Then, they wouldn't need to see each other again for a while.

He was thankful for that. The sooner Riley George was relegated to the past, the better.

"I guess that wraps things up." Travis stood.

"I suppose so." Riley stood, too, and gathered her things. "I passed by the old café on my walk this morning. Are there any plans for it?"

"One day, I hope to reopen it as a Traverser Southern fusion restaurant." He'd admitted that only to Chef Henri.

"But our priority is continuing to update the main building, spa and cottages. Plus, the brewery will be opening soon."

"How much would you need to make the necessary updates *and* open the restaurant?"

Was she hoping they'd finish more renovations before her event?

"We probably need to put another half mil into this place. I'd spend about the same converting the old café into a state-of-the-art restaurant by expanding the footprint of the building and bringing everything up to date."

"Are you looking for investors?" Riley asked.

His gut tightened in response to her question. "I'm considering it, but my dad isn't on board with bringing in investors. I'm still trying to wear him down. Why?"

"I might know someone interested in the opportunity." Riley shrugged. "I'll keep you posted. See you next week."

Riley left the room, her sweet scent trailing in her wake.

Travis's wayward eyes followed the sway of her hips as she exited the room. He groaned. He'd have to deal with Riley for a few more weeks. Then he could go back to forgetting he'd ever met her.

Seven

Riley took another bite of the creamy, delicious cranberry crème brûlée dessert that was the final sample of the menu Travis had developed for her event at their meeting one week earlier.

The entire presentation had been fantastic, and everything from the cranberry orange roast duck and filet mignon to the duchess potatoes and oysters Rockefeller was absolutely divine. She would never admit it to her beloved Chef Henri, but Travis's menu was definitely an upgrade. The guests were going to love the new selections.

They hadn't sent out formal notice that Travis was headlining the event, but the news had been leaked. The charity's office had been receiving daily calls inquiring if it was true. Without even making the formal announcement, ticket sales had increased.

Henri had been right. Making Travis Holloway the

star of the event was a brilliant move. They'd easily sell out the larger venue. She glanced over to Travis a few feet away on a call.

"All right, Pops. I'll see you and Giada for dinner about seven." Travis held up a finger, indicating he'd be with her momentarily. "Thanks. Love you, too."

Travis ended the call and joined her at the table, looking as scrumptious as the food he'd prepared. The crisp white chef's jacket and hat gleamed against his satiny, dark brown skin.

"So what's the verdict?" Travis asked.

"Everything was phenomenal." Riley finished the last spoonful of her cranberry crème brûlée. She should be stuffed. Yet, she'd be willing to arm wrestle her own grandmother for another serving of that creamy deliciousness. "You certainly live up to the hype."

"You doubted it?" Travis chuckled. He removed his hat and stuffed it in his pocket. "Any changes?"

"No, I wouldn't change a thing."

"Excellent. My publicist has been creating some buzz for the event with some of the networks. She'll connect with your PR person to iron out the details. If you need me for anything else, you have my number." Travis stood again. "Enjoy your stay."

"Travis, wait." Riley grabbed his wrist. He tensed, and she released it. Which didn't bode well for the proposal she'd practiced on her drive up from Charlotte that morning.

"Is there something else?" His voice was tight.

"Yes. Could we take a walk? I'd like to show you something."

Travis checked his watch—something he did constantly around her. "I have half an hour before my meeting with the catering manager."

They made their way through the lobby, across the lawn and toward the lake.

"If this is about decorations or changes to the grounds, that's a conversation for Molly and our groundskeeper, Milo."

"It isn't." Riley's stomach knotted.

"Then what is this about?" Travis pressed as they made their way toward the lake.

"I need you to have an open mind about this."

"About what?" Travis was increasingly tense.

"I've been thinking about your dream of reinventing the old café as a signature Traverser restaurant." She gestured toward the building. "It's a brilliant idea, Travis. I'd love to see the place open by this time next year."

"So would I." He studied the building longingly.

The old place held lots of fond memories for Riley. She could only imagine how much it would mean to Travis to open one of his signature restaurants there.

"Like I said, our focus is on making updates to the property first." Travis turned back to her. "We're all already pretty heavily invested in the place, and in our own businesses. So short of one of us winning the lottery, it ain't happening. Not right now."

A slow smile spread across Riley's face. "I can help with that."

"You found an investor?"

"You could say that." Riley's heart beat rapidly, and her throat felt dry.

"Who?"

"Me."

His expression of anticipation crumpled, then transformed into a frown.

Not the reaction I was hoping for.

"Not a good idea, Princess," he said. "No, scratch that. It's an absolutely *terrible* idea."

"What difference does it make if it's me or some random investor whom you seemed perfectly happy to accept money from?"

His nostrils flared. "We both know the answer to that, Riley."

"You're not even going to listen to my offer before you reject it?"

"No," Travis said emphatically. He turned and walked back toward the main building as she scrambled to keep up with his long stride in her four-inch, black-and-silver, Italian-made Kendall Miles slingback Siren pumps. A wardrobe choice she currently regretted.

"You're not being fair," Riley huffed.

"To whom?" He stopped suddenly and swung around. She nearly slammed into him. "To *you*? Because the George family has always been so fair to everyone they've dealt with, I'm sure." His tone dripped with warranted sarcasm.

Riley cringed inwardly. There had definitely been times when her father and grandfather had been complete assholes to get what they wanted. And the way she'd treated Travis… She hadn't been much different.

"You're not being fair to your dad or to Mack and Grey. To the employees here at Moonlight Ridge. Because, though you've made some improvements, if things don't turn around quickly, we both know the future of the resort is in jeopardy." Riley stood taller when his expression softened. "Are you really going to risk everyone's future just to spite me?"

"I'll find other investors. I just need time."

"Why? When I'm right here offering to give you what you need to complete the renovations *and* open the restaurant."

That got his attention. He stared at her, as if considering it. But then seemed to think better of it.

"I'm not interested in going into business with the George family," Travis said coolly. "That clear enough for you?"

Before he could turn and walk away again, Riley grasped his arm. She stood in front of him, unintimidated by his scowl. "This deal would be strictly between you and me, Travis."

"I suppose you think that's more appealing." He laughed bitterly. "It isn't. I remember how this goes, Princess. And I won't risk you pulling the rug on this deal when you suddenly lose interest."

"I deserve that, and I can understand why you're hesitant to trust me, Travis. But I was a kid then. We both were." Riley's eyes searched his, her heart racing. "I can't fix what happened then. But I can help Moonlight Ridge now. Please, at least hear me out."

"Look, I appreciate that you want to make amends or something, Rye." He used the affectionate nickname he'd called her when they were dating.

It gave her a little hope.

"But it would be better if we dealt with someone I don't have a rocky personal history with. Besides, I know you're saying this deal would be between us, and I hate to sound grim, but if something happened to you while you held a stake in the property, as part of your estate, that stake would go to your family. That's a risk I'm not willing to take."

"What if I didn't want a stake in the property?"

"I'm supposed to believe you'd hand over the cash expecting nothing in return?"

"I would need something in return. It just wouldn't be a stake in the property."

Travis stared at her through narrowed slits, his arms folded. "What do you want, Riley?"

She lifted her chin and met his gaze. "A husband."

He stared at her a moment, as if he couldn't possibly have heard her right. Then he broke into laughter that began as a quiet chuckle but escalated to a deep belly laugh that had him nearly doubled over. Travis laughed so hard he nearly went into a coughing fit.

"You've got jokes, I see, Princess." He wiped his eyes, still laughing. "For a hot second, I thought you might be serious."

"I *am* serious." Riley folded her arms. "You need a million dollars. I need a husband for one year."

"Rich people." Travis shook his head, as if he himself didn't fit that description. "You think the rules don't apply to you. That you can do whatever the hell you want. I'm not a mail-order husband, sweetheart. But I'm sure you can find yourself one for a lot less."

"I'm not trying to buy you. I need your help. We'd be helping each other. Just walk with me. I'll explain."

Travis stared at her for what felt like forever. Just when she was sure he was going to tell her to go to hell, he sighed. "Let's sit on the bench there. Your feet must be killing you."

"They are." She was more aware of the pain now that he'd mentioned it. "Thank you."

They sat on the bench and Riley explained the parameters of her grandfather's will and why she needed a husband for one year to gain full control of her trust.

He listened carefully as he stared out onto the lake. "There has to be some loophole. Have you checked with a lawyer?"

"I had a team of *very* expensive, highly rated lawyers working on this for the past few months. Grandad's will is ironclad." She sighed. "It was one of those overpriced lawyers who recommended that I strike a mutually beneficial deal with 'a man of means.'"

Travis rubbed his stubbled chin as he stared out onto the placid water. "I can appreciate your dilemma. But why ask me?" He turned toward her. "I'm sure your rich playboy friends would be falling over themselves to strike up a deal like this."

"I'd rather forfeit my inheritance than spend the next year pretend-married to any of those self-centered jerks." Riley shuddered at the possibility.

"Sounds like you should choose better friends, Princess."

"That's what I'm *trying* to do."

"Oh, so you're not just trying to buy a pretend husband. You expect us to be friends, too?" He was mocking her and enjoying every moment of it.

But as long as he was actively involved in the conversation, he was considering it.

"I'm not trying to buy *you*, Travis. I'm buying your cooperation with a *mutually* beneficial deal. It's essentially free money. No other investor is going to hand you a deal as sweet as this."

Travis's dark eyes lingered on her mouth. "It's not exactly free, Princess. You're asking me to give up an entire year of my dating life."

"You'd just be my husband on paper," Riley countered. "I'd append your last name to mine, but we wouldn't be sleeping together. We wouldn't even need to live together necessarily. And I suppose, as long as you were discreet about it—"

"I don't fuck around with married women, so if I'm wearing a ring and claiming to be your husband, I'm not hooking up with anyone else. And since we wouldn't be sleeping together, what you're asking me to do is go a year without. That's a mighty big ask."

"I realize that," Riley said. "But it would be worth it. You'd get to do all of the additional improvements here without spending a dime of your own cash or giving up a stake in the place."

"You're talking a year from now. I need to continue the momentum Mack and Grey have built *now*." Travis stood abruptly, as if he'd heard enough. She sensed he'd lost whatever interest he might've had in the deal. "Thank you for your very generous but unusual offer. But I'll take my chances with a *traditional* investor."

"I'll give you half the money up front." Riley shot to her feet, too, and grasped his elbow. "That way you can keep moving forward with your improvements. You'd get the rest on our one-year anniversary."

"It's a tempting offer, RG. But—"

"You don't have to answer today. Just think about it. *Please.*" Riley hated sounding so desperate. "Talk it over with your dad and brothers. This involves them, too."

"They wouldn't be the ones giving up sex for a year, would they?"

"No, they wouldn't. But I'm sure they'd be eternally grateful to you for doing this."

"Too bad that won't keep me warm on a cold night." Travis's dark eyes glinted in the sunlight.

"I'll buy you a year's supply of Vaseline and a subscription to the adult cable channel of your choice," Riley teased.

"I already have both." Travis winked. "Tell me the truth. Are you asking me to do this just to piss off your parents?"

"I consider that icing on the cake." Riley shrugged.

She'd taken pleasure in anticipating her parents' reaction when she announced she'd be marrying Travis Holloway. It would be like their dismayed reaction when she'd told them Travis would be the featured chef at their charity gala…but times ten.

"While I'd get a kick out of playing *Guess Who's Coming to Dinner* with your parents, a year of that shit is not my idea of a good time. Thanks anyway, Princess. Now, unless you have any other indecent proposals, I have a meeting in about five minutes, and I don't want to be late for it. Good luck on your husband hunt," Travis called over his shoulder as he trotted back to the main building.

Riley palmed her forehead and groaned.

Well, that went well.

This was a long shot, she realized. Still, the fact that Travis Holloway had *zero* interest in her offer, despite her million-dollar bribe, had taken a sledgehammer to her ego. Especially since she was still mildly attracted to him.

Okay, that was a lie. She was *very* attracted to him.

Yes, there were lots of other possibilities who would happily accept her offer. But she didn't want or trust any of them.

Her grandfather's will hadn't left her any choice as to *how* she'd secure her inheritance. But at least she got to decide with whom. And Travis Holloway was the only man she could possibly imagine doing this with. So she wasn't prepared to take her ball and go home. Not yet.

Time to play hardball.

Eight

Travis ended a videoconference with a producer friend and a cooking network exec. Both had been excited about getting behind a limited run reality show that followed the revitalization of Moonlight Ridge. They'd discussed the next steps and would send a camera crew out the following week to begin capturing footage.

He stretched in his chair, his legs and back aching from a long, busy day—most of which he'd spent on his feet. Travis was pleased with Hallie's progress. He understood now why his father wouldn't give up on her. She had the potential to be a really good chef.

She was independent and yes, she could be a smart-ass, but he liked her. More important, she was self-aware enough to recognize her need for improvement. And she soaked up everything he taught her like a sponge.

"Ready to shut it down for the night?" Mack stood in the doorway suddenly.

"Just about." Travis kneaded the knot he sometimes got in his neck from looking down while he cooked. In LA he'd taken up hot yoga. It felt like torture, at first. But it eased the tension and the aches and pains he often experienced. Some of it was occupational. Some of it was lingering repercussions from his catastrophic injuries in the crash.

Maybe he'd find a yoga studio around town.

Mack sat in front of his desk. "How's everything going with Hallie and Ross?"

"Things are going great with Hallie. Ross is a little more resistant," Travis said.

"Will he be a problem?" Mack raised an eyebrow.

"Nah." Travis shook his head. "Ross just needs a minute to adjust. He'll be fine."

"And how are the plans for the new menu coming?"

"Great, actually. Also…" Travis leaned forward, his elbows on the desk "…I've been considering converting the old café into a Traverser restaurant."

"A signature Traverser restaurant plus the brewery? That could really put Moonlight Ridge on the map again. What kind of timeline are you looking at?"

"Not sure." Travis shrugged. "Our focus has to be completing renovations on the resort. What's the point in drawing people here if the amenities are outdated?"

"I'm sure Grey would agree," Mack said. "But then again, I jumped right into opening the brewery before the renovations were done."

"What would I agree with?" Grey popped his head into the doorway, his dark blue eyes twinkling with mischief.

"Still a nosy, eavesdropping busybody, huh?" Mack furrowed one brow.

Travis laughed. He missed moments like this with his brothers. Since he'd returned to Moonlight Ridge, the tension that had knotted his gut whenever he was around Mack or Grey had dissipated.

They'd even fallen back into the habit of giving each other shit without anyone taking offense. He and Grey more than Mack, who'd always been Mr. Serious. Still, Mack was making an effort to let down his guard, and Travis appreciated that.

"I heard my name while passing by." Grey sat beside Mack. "What are you two up to?"

"I'm waiting on Molly. She's finishing up a meeting with Ross about the charity event we're doing for Travis's girlfriend." Mack smirked.

"Riley isn't my girlfriend, and you know it." Travis organized the papers on his desk.

"I heard you were doing an event for your ex. How'd that happen? I thought you hated her." Grey scooted to the edge of his chair.

"I never hated her." Travis sighed. "Was I devastated by what she did? Hell yeah. Have I forgotten that shit? No. But I also don't blame her for what happened that night." Travis looked at Mack, who'd been driving the truck. "Nor you," he added before turning to Grey. "Or you."

His brothers stiffened slightly, then nodded. Both of them seemed relieved he'd finally said the thing he hadn't been able to say all those years ago. That he didn't blame either of them or Riley for what had happened to him.

Something he should've said long ago.

But back then, he'd been too angry to let any of them

off the hook. He was in physical and mental agony. And he'd wanted them to feel a little of that pain, too.

"Maybe you don't blame her, but part of me does. I still can't believe she had the audacity to show up to the hospital afterward," Mack grumbled.

"It took guts for her to show up there." Grey ran a hand through his thick brown hair. "She could've walked away and not looked back or just sent flowers. But she came to the hospital, devastated and desperate to see Travis. When you refused to see her, she kept calling to check on you." Grey shrugged his narrow shoulders. "Seemed like genuine concern to me."

"Enough talk about Riley, okay?" Travis said. "First Chef H ambushes me with a request to headline her event, strongly hinting that we should move it here. Then I keep having to meet with her. And today she actually asked me to *marry* her." Travis still couldn't believe it.

Grey broke into laughter. Mack didn't.

His elder brother tilted his head, one eyebrow raised. "Please tell me you're kidding."

"I'm dead serious."

"Wait, I thought you were joking," Grey said mid-laugh. "You're serious?"

"Yes!" Travis said again, irritated. "Is it that remarkable that a woman would ask me to marry her? I get at least three marriage proposals a week in my fan mail, you know."

"Yes, it's remarkable." Mack steepled his hands. "Especially when it's the George family heiress who proposed to you. Has she had a thing for you all this time?"

"This wasn't a romantic proposal. It was a business one." Travis explained Riley's situation and why she was looking for a temporary husband.

Grey whistled. "That's unbelievably sexist. Is it even legally binding?"

"According to the expensive lawyers she enlisted, it was the old man's money. He can distribute it however he sees fit. Even if it makes him a controlling misogynist from beyond the grave." Travis shrugged.

"So she needs this marriage to claim her inheritance." Mack rubbed his chin thoughtfully. "What is she offering in exchange?"

Travis tapped his thumb on the desk blotter. "To finance the remaining renovations at Moonlight Ridge, including enough to transform the old café into a state-of-the-art Traverser restaurant."

"Shit." Mack covered his open mouth. "That's one hell of an incentive."

"And you turned that down?" Grey asked incredulously. "You wanted to raise cash, Pops is against outside investors and we're all tapped out with our personal investments. But if you marry Riley, problem solved. We'd be keeping it in the family." Grey's dark blue eyes danced.

His brother was enjoying this way too much.

"You are so fucking unfunny." Travis tossed a balled-up piece of paper at Grey's head.

Grey swatted the paper missile down and disintegrated into laughter. "Would you have to take her last name? I mean, it only seems fair since she asked you."

"I knew I shouldn't have told you two." Travis dragged a hand down his face.

"C'mon, T, I'm just kidding." Grey chuckled. "Don't be so sensitive."

"I'm not being sensitive," Travis shot back. "You're being an ass."

"You're awful quiet about this." Grey turned to Mack.

Their older brother grunted and rubbed his chin. "I don't like that she thinks she can just waltz in here and buy herself a husband. Besides, hasn't Riley done enough already?"

"I told you, I don't hold her or anyone responsible for what happened. We were all just kids." The tension was rising in Travis's neck again. "But I do think her lingering guilt is part of the reason she's offering such a favorable deal."

"Then I say let her do it." Grey wasn't joking.

"And give the Georges a stake in Moonlight Ridge?" Mack asked. "Over my dead body."

"I said the same thing," Travis told him. "But this deal would be strictly between her and me, and she doesn't want a stake in Moonlight Ridge."

Mack's eyes widened. He leaned forward with his elbows on his knees. "So she's just gonna hand over the money, no strings attached? No way." He answered his own question.

"It's true." Travis shrugged. "She's willing to draw up a contract explicitly stating as much. But it wouldn't exactly be *free* money. I'd have to stay married to her for an entire year."

"A year is a long time to be tethered to someone you don't even like." Grey tilted his head. "Or are you still into her?"

Heat traveled up Travis's neck and his throat suddenly felt dry.

How did he answer that?

"No, I'm not 'into' Riley."

"But you are attracted to her." Mack said the quiet

part out loud. The part Travis thought he'd been clever enough to conceal.

"That's immaterial," Travis said. "The marriage would be in name only, so I'd be giving up sex and dating for a year. Because despite what she insinuated, I'm not telling the world she and I are together and then creeping all over town. Not my style."

"Good move." Mack nodded approvingly. "With your visibility, there's no way that wouldn't blow back on you. She'd come out looking like the sweet, angelic heiress who'd been done wrong, and you'd forever be the bad boy who cheated on her."

"Exactly." Travis turned to his computer when it dinged, indicating he'd received another email. He'd had his fill of those for the day.

"Also, Pops would never buy a marriage on paper," Grey said. "So if you're going to do this, it needs to be legit. That means living together, eating together, sleeping together. That's also the only way he'll accept Riley's money."

"Why are you talking like this is an actual thing he plans to do?" Mack asked.

"Because now that you two are locked down in relationships, he can't stand to see me happily unattached," Travis said. He checked his email. "Speak of the devil."

"An email from the future Mrs. Holloway?" Grey raised his eyebrows and smirked.

"Shut. Up." Travis gritted the words out between clenched teeth. This time Mack laughed, too. Travis opened Riley's message. "Wow."

"What is it?" Mack's voice was laced with concern. "Is she pressuring you?"

"You could say that." Travis fell back against the chair,

one hand clamped over his mouth. "She's upping the deal."

"How much?" Grey asked.

"Another 100K, payable on the day of the wedding And even if things blew up the very next day, I wouldn't have to return it." Travis scanned the bullet points in her concise email.

"She *really* wants this. With you," Mack added. "Because I'm sure she could find some guy who would've qualified and is willing. I'm not sure if that makes me feel better or worse about the deal."

"Now *you're* talking like this is something I should actually do," Travis said. "Both of you have lost it."

"Any other incentives to sweeten the pot? A Tesla for your favorite brother or a house at the beach, maybe?" Grey joked.

"Neither." Travis stared at the screen.

"But she is offering *something*," Mack said.

It wasn't a question, and Travis was equally comforted and annoyed that Mack still knew him so well.

"She respects that I'm not down with hooking up with someone else during our fake union, so she's offering to…*consummate* the marriage."

He felt ridiculous using that word instead of saying what it really meant: *sex*. Riley was willing to take the relationship where it hadn't gone before…to the bedroom.

"Wow. She really does want you." Grey echoed Mack's earlier sentiment.

The three of them sat together in silence. Finally, Mack said, "You should consider it."

"A minute ago, you were pissed she'd come in here and tried to buy herself a husband." He parroted Mack's earlier words, mimicking his voice and making Grey chuckle.

"I know. But this is a pretty damn good payday for spending a year in the company of a beautiful woman you're totally into anyway," Mack said.

"So now I've graduated from being a long-term male escort to a straight-up gigolo." Travis shook his head. "Well, at least I'm moving up in the world."

"It's not like that." Grey's voice was more serious now. "I hate how Riley ended things between you two and that it triggered an unfortunate chain of events. But the truth is that we've always liked Riley. She was a genuinely decent human being who was nothing like her stuck-up family. Her behavior that night was an anomaly."

It was true. Even before he'd shown an interest in Riley, he'd liked her. She was sweet, thoughtful, funny. And she'd never treated them or any of the staff as if they were beneath her. But sometimes people changed, and not always for the better.

"Or maybe she finally showed us who she really was." Travis frowned.

"You don't really believe that," Grey said.

"What I believe doesn't matter." Travis shut the lid to his laptop, sliding it into his bag. "Now, I'm getting out of here. I suggest you two do the same."

Travis said his goodbyes, then took a golf cart back to his cottage. But he couldn't get the photos Riley sent out of his head. She hadn't sent some racy photo to entice him. Instead, she'd attached old selfies she'd taken on her cell phone. One was a sweet shot of him kissing her cheek while she stared at the camera, her eyes and mouth widened in surprise.

The second photo was of him holding her in his arms

as they stood by the lake at sunset. She gazed up at him lovingly as he leaned down to kiss her. It was a photo Grey had taken.

Travis hadn't told his brothers about the photos. And he'd tried to hide the feelings they stirred in his chest. Those moments with Riley were branded into his memory. No matter how much he'd tried to forget them.

Travis was starving after his long day at work and running a few miles around the lake. He'd taken a hot shower, gotten dressed and made it over to his dad's place—the house where he, Mack and Grey had grown up. He was having dinner with his dad and his live-in caretaker, Giada, who'd once worked for Moonlight Ridge as a housekeeper before leaving to become a nurse. Maybe they'd play a few games of billiards. He might even let the old man win.

He made his way up the steps of the wide, wraparound porch. It was a lovely end-of-summer day in the Blue Ridge Mountains. The temperature was mild, and his father's front door was open to permit the fresh mountain breeze to blow in through the screen door.

There was laughter inside. Travis knocked and his father's two golden retrievers, Trouble and Nonsense, met him at the door, their tails wagging.

"It's open. Come on in, son," his father called out to him.

Travis opened the door and stooped to pet his father's companions. Then he followed the heavenly scent of Italian food. His belly rumbled. Giada was an excellent cook. Whatever she'd made would be delicious.

"Hey, Pops." Travis nodded toward his father, seated in his favorite chair. "Hey, Gi—"

Travis stopped in his tracks. His jaw dropped. "Riley? What are you… *Why* are you here?"

"That's no way to greet a young lady, son." Jameson eyed him.

"Sorry, I was just surprised to see Riley here." Travis ran a hand over his close-cropped hair. His eyes locked with hers. "Hey, Riley. Good to see you *again*."

"Hi, Travis." Riley gave him an innocent little finger wave that made him want to both scream and kiss her.

Kiss her? Where the hell did that come from?

What he wanted was for Riley George to get out of his spot on his dad's sofa and out of his father's house. But Jameson Holloway wasn't above grounding Travis and sending him to his old room if he said so.

So instead, he sucked in a deep breath, cleansing any ridiculous thoughts of kissing her from his brain. Then he released the breath and forced a polite smile as he stared her down.

Riley George, what the hell kind of game are you playing?

Nine

Riley watched Travis do what she was pretty sure was some yogic deep breathing, which meant he was probably pretty furious at her for crashing his dinner plans with his dad.

But desperate times called for desperate measures.

Riley didn't need access to her full trust for herself. She lived a comfortable life with her salary and the monthly stipend from her trust. Plus, she had a healthy savings. No, she needed that money because two of the organizations she supported personally had lost the government funding that was the linchpin of their very existence.

Neither organization met the established criteria to receive funding from her family's foundation. And both had maybe enough money in reserve to struggle through another year or so before going under. She needed to secure that money to help fund both organizations while they sought alternate, sustainable funding sources.

So here she sat on the cozy, well-worn sofa of Jameson Holloway, a man she admired and had always been very fond of, hoping to convince his son to marry her for money.

Wow. Even in my head that sounds pathetic.

Travis sank onto the opposite end of the sofa and studied her carefully. "What brings you here, Riley? Did we forget something in today's meeting?"

His father's deep baritone chuckle drew both of their attention.

"Riley isn't here to see you, son. She didn't even know you were coming until we invited her to stay for dinner. She came here to see your old man." Jameson winked at him. "No need to be jealous."

"My bad, Pops." Travis grinned at his father, then gave her a knowing look.

"Riley was telling me about that cranberry crème brûlée you made for her today. Had my mouth watering." Jameson chuckled and climbed to his feet, ignoring the cane Giada had made a point of setting beside his chair before she'd gone to the kitchen to finish dinner.

"I'd planned to bring you some, but the kitchen staff crushed the leftovers." Travis watched his father shuffle toward the fireplace mantel.

"Sounds like it's a hit, son. Let's add it to the holiday menu."

"You've got it." When Travis pulled out his phone and opened it, the photo of their first kiss filled the screen.

He'd read her email, and that photo was the last thing he'd been looking at before he'd arrived.

Hope stirred in Riley's chest, and her heart beat faster. When she glanced up, Travis's eyes met hers.

He closed the photo and typed something into his phone before putting it back into his pocket. Travis turned toward his father, who was flipping through a photo album.

"Is there something I can help you find?" Travis walked over to his father.

"No, I'm just… Here they are," Jameson said gleefully. He lifted the plastic sheet and pulled out two photos. He handed one to Travis, then held the other out to Riley.

She walked over to him and took the photo from his hand.

"This is me." She turned to Jameson, who watched her with a warm grin that made her heart dance.

"Sure is." He chuckled, moving back toward his chair. He sat down with some effort. "And that's Travis standing right there next to you. I think at the time he might've been ten or eleven. You were a bit younger."

"This was one of the children's day events you all used to have here." Riley walked over to Travis and showed him the photo. In the picture, the two of them stood together with about twenty other kids of hotel guests and employees. "I hadn't seen this photo before."

Travis nodded to acknowledge the photo, then stared at the one in his hand.

"Is that from the same day?" Riley asked.

"No, that's a photo of you at one of the dances we had here," Jameson said. "More accurately, it's a photo of my son here mooning over you like some lost puppy." He chuckled. "The boy was head over heels for you from that moment on."

Travis glanced over at his father, then at her.

Her cheeks heated. Chef H had known about their clandestine relationship. But it seemed Jameson hadn't been oblivious to their feelings for each other, after all.

"I remember that night." Travis's voice was faint, his expression wistful.

Riley couldn't help wondering what Travis was thinking now and what he'd been thinking the night that photo had been snapped.

Travis handed the photo to her. "You never said what brought you here this evening."

"I couldn't come here two weekends in a row without stopping in to visit your dad."

"And she brought the loveliest bouquet of flowers and a warm apple pie." Giada's accented voice floated into the room ahead of her.

The older woman's long dark hair was swept up in a neat bun. She wore an apron over her dress. Her dark eyes shone as she grinned at Riley.

"Did she?" Travis studied her with one brow hiked. "Well, that certainly was thoughtful of her, wasn't it?"

"It was indeed." Giada squeezed Riley's arm.

"My most vivid memory of your dad is him rearranging the flowers in the front lobby." Riley shrugged. "I was driving past a florist, and I saw this arrangement. It reminded me of that. I'd planned to pop in to see your dad anyway, so it seemed like fate." She ignored the heat that crawled over her skin beneath his assessing gaze.

"Well, dinner is ready. I made my famous eggplant Parmesan, so I hope you're both hungry," Giada said.

"Sounds fabulous," Riley said. "May I use your restroom first?"

"Of course," Jameson said. "It's just down the hall there."

"Meet us in the dining room when you're done," Giada called after her.

Riley went to the restroom, as much to escape Travis's heated stare as to wash her hands for dinner. When she emerged from the bathroom, Travis was standing in the hallway.

"Did you follow me to the bathroom?"

"What are you doing here, Riley?" he asked again. "If this is about your crazy-ass marriage proposal, leave my father out of it."

Travis placed a hand on the wall above her and leaned closer. Her heart thumped in her chest as his clean, woodsy scent surrounded her. Suddenly, it was much harder to breathe.

"Was I not clear about that?" she asked flippantly. "I'm here to see your dad. You know how much I've always liked him."

"So much that you haven't been in contact in over fifteen years." Travis's nostrils flared.

"Before I started planning this gala, I hadn't been to Asheville in fifteen years," Riley said. "Our events are usually held in Charlotte."

Travis glared at her. "So this has nothing to do with your offer or the fact that you heard me saying I'd be here tonight?"

"Maybe that, too," she admitted. "But I would've come to see your father regardless."

"Did you tell him about your offer?"

"Of course not. I think you should consult with him before rejecting my offer out of hand, but I wouldn't take the proposal to him myself. I'm not that manipulative."

"But you are trying to manipulate me into accepting your deal?"

Riley held up her thumb and forefinger, peeking through them. "Maybe the *tiniest* bit."

Travis removed his hand from the wall and stepped back. He folded his arms and his sleeves pulled tight over his thick biceps.

Riley held back an involuntary whimper.

Lord, have mercy.

Travis looked good and smelled enticing. And when she'd put her hand on his arm earlier that day, his strong, muscled bicep had felt so solid. She couldn't help wondering how it would feel to have those strong arms circling her waist. Or to press her lips to his.

"I'm the one who'll decide whether or not I do this. Appealing to my dad is only gonna piss me off," he said. "Got it?"

Riley nodded, her heart thudding. "I just wanted to be here in case your dad had questions. To reassure him of—"

"Your intentions for his son?" Travis lifted a brow.

"Something like that." She shrugged, then asked, "Does this mean you're considering—"

"I don't know what I'm thinking right now." Travis seemed irritated. He drew in a slow breath. "But if we do this, and that's a huge, monumental-sized *if*, we can't tell my dad about this arrangement."

"You want me to lie to him?" Riley really liked Jameson. She wasn't comfortable misleading him.

"It won't be a lie." Travis's stare set her body on fire. His arms dropped to his sides. "My dad obviously knows how we felt about each other back then. Since he went through all the trouble of digging out those photos and asking you to stay for dinner… He probably thinks he's slick with his not-so-subtle matchmaking."

"So that's why he showed us those photos." She smiled. It was sweet that Jameson wanted to see them together.

"So we tell him that seeing each other again stirred up some old feelings," he said.

Riley shifted her weight from one foot to the other as Travis stepped closer in the narrow hallway. "Definitely true."

"Good," he said. "Then maybe we spend the next month or so getting to know each other. If we can make it through a couple of months without strangling each other, we'll see where things go from there."

"I'm grateful you're considering my offer," she said. "But could we accelerate the timeline? I was hoping we could elope to Vegas maybe. And soon."

"I appreciate your dilemma," Travis said coolly. "But surely you can appreciate mine. I'm not spending a year of my life tied to someone I can't stand being in the same room with. So before I'll agree to this deal, I need to know that we're compatible enough to make a long-term, *nonsexual* relationship work." He stressed the word and her heart deflated a little.

Was he not attracted to her? Riley was sure she'd seen him checking her out on more than one occasion. At Henri's. At the lake. And just now, she was sure that there'd been heat in his dark eyes as they'd taken her in. She'd offered a bona fide, *consummated* marriage.

So why was he insistent that sex was off the table?

"Just take a breath and—"

Travis was midsentence when Riley stepped forward, clutched the soft fabric of his button-down shirt and lifted onto her toes. She pressed her mouth to his and he stiffened.

She cradled his whiskered chin, kissing him again. And again.

After the third kiss, Travis's arms slipped around her waist. He backed her against the wall, his lips gliding over hers. Travis angled her head, deepening their kiss as his warm tongue slipped between her lips.

Riley sighed softly, her eyes closed as her fingertips drifted to his back.

"Ahem."

They were both startled as they turned toward the petite woman who stood there smiling.

"Sorry to interrupt your…reunion," Giada said. "But your father needs to eat, and we wouldn't think of starting without you."

"Of course. We're sorry." Riley's face flamed with heat as she stepped away from Travis and straightened her shirt.

Giada looked at Travis then circled her mouth, indicating the colored gloss all over his.

He nodded his thanks, then stepped inside the bathroom.

"See you two in a sec. Then after dinner…have at it." Giada grinned before heading back up the hall.

Riley sighed, her heart still racing from the kiss that had set her entire body on fire and left her wanting much more from the man she'd asked to be her fake husband.

Travis washed and dried his hands before stepping into the hall and looking around.

"Giada went back to the dining room," Riley assured him as she leaned against the wall.

The sensation of how it had felt to be pinned between Travis's hard body and the wall sent a fresh wave of electricity up her spine.

"Looks like the plan is in motion." Travis ran a hand over his head.

"Excellent. I'll have my lawyer draw up the agreement and get it to your lawyer by the end of next week."

"Fine." Travis nodded stiffly, then held out his open palm to her. "Showtime?"

"Showtime." Riley slipped her hand in his and they walked into the dining room, greeted by wide, knowing grins from Jameson and Giada.

Let the games begin.

Ten

Travis stood in the bedroom of his cottage and rummaged through his closet. Which tie worked best for a dinner date with one's soon-to-be in-laws?

"I'd go with the dark red one." Riley leaned against the doorway. A mischievous grin curved her sensuous mouth, which he'd found himself preoccupied with lately.

"You're supposed to be waiting for me downstairs." He picked up the dark red tie and looped it around his neck.

"We need to talk."

"I know. I haven't signed the papers yet." He knotted the tie.

It'd been two weeks since Riley had kissed him at his dad's house. Two weeks since they'd been pretend dating. But he hadn't agreed to the marriage. Only to think about it.

And it was still very much a *maybe*.

"That's not what I was going to say." Riley trained her dark brown eyes on his as she tightened the knot, straightened his tie then smoothed it down his chest. His skin danced with electricity beneath her touch, even through his clothing.

"We haven't discussed our living arrangements," she said.

Travis lifted his gray suit jacket from the bed. He hadn't permitted himself to think that far ahead. But it was a pretty damn important question. Especially since Grey had pointed out that the two of them needed to live together if they had any chance of making Jameson believe they were really a couple.

"I certainly can't help run Moonlight Ridge from your place in Charlotte," he noted. "But I imagine you can't run the foundation from here, either. So where does that leave us?"

Riley took the jacket from him and held it up as he slipped one arm, then the other, inside.

"The situation isn't ideal, but I can create a satellite office and work virtually from here. I can drive into the office a couple of times a week from here or Atlanta," she said. "You're the one doing me a favor, so it only seems fair that I'm the one who has to make the sacrifice."

"Will your family go for that?"

"I run the foundation. Besides, as long as the work is getting done, what does it matter where I'm working from?" She seemed to bristle at the implication she needed her parents' approval to work remotely.

"You'd be willing to move in here with me?" Travis glanced around the cottage.

The twelve-hundred-square-foot shabby-chic bungalow was in need of renovation. Perfect for an unpretentious bachelor who used it to sleep and change clothing between activities. But a lot less appealing for an investment heiress who was accustomed to the best.

Riley followed his gaze around the room, but her mouth curved in a soft smile. "It's adorable," she said. "With a few tweaks here and there, the place will look great."

That hadn't been the reaction he expected at all. He'd expected her to insist they move into one of the renovated cottages or rent something nicer off the estate.

Point one for Riley.

Actually, that wasn't true. Riley had impressed him in a number of ways in the past few weeks. He wasn't surprised she was running the George Family Foundation. She'd always been kind and empathetic. She'd been the most relatable person in her family.

But in the past few weeks, he'd gotten to see her working with some of the charities up close. She hadn't shown up in an expensive suit and shoes, smiled for the camera and handed over a check. Riley had arrived in sweats, sneakers and an old T-shirt. She rolled up her sleeves and went to work.

He'd seen her dig in the dirt and shovel fertilizer while planting spinach, lettuce and greens in the winter garden at a homeless shelter. She'd helped unload a truck and washed dishes at a women's shelter. All of it had taken him by surprise. But he'd been most impressed with how truly genuine Riley was with the people she dealt with.

She'd been sweet and gregarious as she chatted with a group of homeless men who were absolutely charmed by her. She'd held babies and wiped their little noses so their mothers could have an uninterrupted meal and a little time to themselves at the women's shelter.

The employees and clients of those agencies adored Riley, and he was beginning to see why. But he wouldn't allow that to throw him. This thing between them wasn't real, no matter how hard they sold it. It was a means to an end for both of them.

"So it's settled?" Riley smoothed a hand down his lapels. Her crisp, sweet scent tickled his nostrils. "After the honeymoon, I'll move in here until you're ready to return to Atlanta."

"Honeymoon? Is that really necessary?"

She folded her arms. "Unless you want the entire world to know this is a business arrangement and not a marriage...*yes*."

"We wouldn't be the first busy couple to forgo their honeymoon," Travis complained.

"But it will look awfully suspicious to the world and to my family if we skip it. I wouldn't put it past my father to contest the validity of the marriage."

"Fine," Travis huffed. "Then we'll go on a honeymoon."

"Kind of you to be such a trouper through the hardship of spending a week in the Maldives with..." She smoothed her hands down the sides of her body and turned sideways, showing off her profile. *"...this."*

Travis chuckled. Riley made an excellent point. Most men would fall all over themselves to spend some alone time with the gorgeous heiress. She looked stunning in a dress that clung to her incredible curves. The royal blue fabric looked brilliant against her brown skin. And her legs looked magnificent in her designer heels.

"You do look...amazing."

"Thank you." She curtsied. "You look great, too. Nervous about seeing my parents?"

"It's kind of early in the relationship for the meet-the-parents stage."

"Not when you plan on getting married in a matter of weeks," she countered. "And you didn't answer my question."

"Were you nervous about seeing my dad?" He countered her question with his own.

"No. I was thrilled to see your dad. You know I've always been fond of him."

"That's because my father has always liked you." He didn't need to say the rest. Once her parents realized their little princess had an interest in him, they'd treated him like something they'd tracked into the house on the bottom of their riding boots.

Riley slipped her hand in his. Something she'd first done the night they'd had dinner with his father two weeks earlier.

"I know tonight won't be easy for you, Travis. So I appreciate you doing this for me."

He tugged his hand from hers and buttoned his suit jacket. "It's not a favor, Princess. I'm a husband for hire, remember?"

"Right." Her eyes were filled with disappointment. "Well, I'm grateful, still."

Okay, now he felt like a jerk.

"I haven't signed the agreement yet because I need to know exactly what I'm dealing with here. Personally, I'd get a kick out of pissing off your parents," he admitted. "But I have a brand and a growing empire to protect. I can't afford to get dragged into a contentious, public family squabble."

"My parents won't be happy, but they won't make this messy and public. That isn't their style. They smile on the outside while they quietly plot their revenge. So there's that to look forward to."

"Great."

This just keeps getting better.

Riley slipped her arm through Travis's as they entered the elegant restaurant not far from the Biltmore Estate. They followed the hostess to the table where her parents were seated.

"One more thing," she whispered to Travis. "They had no idea I was bringing you."

"That would explain the shocked look on their faces," he whispered back. "Thanks for the heads up, *Princess*."

"Mom. Dad." Riley tightened her grip on Travis's bicep as they stood in front of the table. "You remember Travis Holloway from our summers at Moonlight Ridge. Before he became a world-famous restaurateur." Riley smiled at Travis with genuine pride. "And Travis, you remember my parents, Ted and Regina George."

"Mr. and Mrs. George." Travis nodded at them. "Pleasure to see you again."

Riley wondered how painful it was for Travis to say those words to her parents. But he was doing it. For her. And a huge sack of money. But she preferred to focus on the former.

"Travis, you've become quite the culinary superstar," her mother said after a few moments of awkward silence. A thin smile spread across her lips. "How nice of you to join us. Please, have a seat." She gestured to the other side of the table.

Riley slipped into the seat across from her mother while Travis sat across from her father, who still hadn't greeted them.

"So, what brings the two of you to town?" Riley asked, knowing full well what had brought her parents to Asheville after all these years.

She'd spent most of the past two weeks staying at Moonlight Ridge, just up the road. And she'd been making a concerted effort to expand the reach of their foundation here in town.

Most of the organizations they worked with were based in Charlotte. But in the two weeks that she'd been here in town, she'd been laying the groundwork to begin funding a few agencies in the surrounding area, including a homeless shelter and a women and children's shelter. And since she'd gotten Travis to volunteer with her at those organizations as part of the PR for the upcoming gala, the news had undoubtedly gotten back to her mother that she was spending lots of time with her former beau. A relationship they hadn't approved of.

Her parents had come here to guilt her into doing what they felt was best for her. Their seating formation was a dead giveaway; they were seated on the same side of the table so they could team up on her and convince her to see things their way.

Travis and her father were still staring each other down in silence. Her father wore a smug look of displeasure while Travis's expression conveyed amused derision.

If she had to declare a winner of their staring contest, it would be Travis by a landslide.

"Ted, you're being ridiculous," her mother whispered loudly as she poked him with her elbow beneath the table. "Say hello to the young man."

"Travis." Her father uttered his name through clenched teeth. "We have some family business to discuss with our daughter, so we weren't expecting you this evening.

Your presence took me by surprise." Her father smoothed a hand over the thinning spot at the back of his head.

"Your daughter is full of surprises this evening." Travis narrowed his gaze at her.

"I wanted my three favorite people in the world to sit down together." Riley slipped her arm through Travis's, ignoring the look of alarm on her parents' faces. "I did what I had to do to make that happen."

"Things are certainly moving quickly," her mother noted. "Didn't you two just reconnect a few weeks ago, when Henri bowed out of the gala?"

"We did," Riley confirmed. "But it didn't take long for us to realize how much we still cared about each other. We've been practically inseparable since then."

Travis draped his arm across the back of her chair. "It's been wonderful getting to know Riley again. She's a truly impressive woman."

His words felt genuine. Her heart swelled as she leaned into him.

Gina George gestured for the server to refill her glass with whatever it was she was drinking. Likely a gin and tonic.

"We're both determined to make up for the time that was stolen from us." Riley glared at her parents, trying to tamp down the anger rising in her chest.

Her parents exchanged a look that was part guilt, part indignation.

"The time you've spent apart has worked out well for both of you." Her father sipped his drink, then set it down. "You've made quite the name for yourself in the food industry, Travis. Between your restaurant business and reality show appearances, I'm surprised you have time to gallivant around Asheville with my daughter."

"My father had a serious health issue a few months ago. My brothers and I are seeing after him and the resort." Travis's body tensed. "So Asheville is my satellite base for now."

"Traverser." Her mother pronounced the word in perfect French, which she spoke fluently. "That's French for *traverse, cross, pass through*. And, I believe, it's the origin of your name." Her mother gauged Travis's reaction.

"That's right." He nodded. "I've gone through a lot in my life to get where I am now. So Traverser seemed like the perfect name for my restaurant group."

"Interesting that you chose to use your given name rather than your family name for your company." Her father shook the ice in his glass.

"Dad!" Riley was angry on Travis's behalf. They'd been there less than ten minutes and already her father had managed to highlight Travis's difficult family situation.

"It's fine, babe." Travis dropped his hand to her waist and tucked her against him as much as their chairs would permit. "I'm not ashamed of being adopted or going through the foster system. Not everyone has the perfect, charmed lives your family has been fortunate enough to enjoy. Some of us aren't just handed a fortune on our twenty-first birthdays, Mr. George. We actually have to hustle and work hard to make something of ourselves."

Touché.

A vein bulged in her father's neck, and his forehead and cheeks flushed.

Riley held back a snort. *Another win for Travis.*

"On that note, perhaps we should order." Her mother glanced nervously between the two men who continued to stare at one another.

"Yes, let's." Riley picked up her menu and handed Travis his. If they had their faces buried in their menus, they couldn't stare each other down.

They ordered dinner and managed to have civil conversation. Mostly owing to her mother's diligent efforts, honed through years of hosting dinner parties, and Riley's continual prompting of Travis to talk about some of his latest accomplishments. It was the most painful hour of conversation Riley had ever endured. She was almost relieved when Travis had to leave the table to take an important call.

"What do you think you're doing, young lady?" her father seethed the moment Travis walked away.

"Trying to eat my dessert in peace," Riley replied sweetly, putting down her fork. "But I guess you're set on ruining that, too."

"What's that supposed to mean?" her father demanded.

"It means I'm thirty-two years old and I'm sick to death of you trying to dictate what I do and whom I do it with." Riley folded her arms on the table. "So if this is the part where you forbid me to see Travis again, save it, Dad. It won't work this time."

"Riley Anne George—"

"What your father means, sweetie," her mother cooed, halting him with a well-placed hand on his arm, "is that you have such a big heart. It's what makes you the perfect person to head up the foundation. But when it comes to matters of the heart, your propensity for seeing the good in everyone can sometimes be a liability."

"Mom, I appreciate your concern, but I'm not an impressionable teenage girl. I'm a grown woman." Riley's voice slowly elevated, her frustration rising.

Diners at two nearby tables looked over, but Riley

didn't care. She'd had enough of her parents' meddling in her life.

"There's no need to cause a scene, missy," her mother whispered loudly, her cheeks crimson as her eyes shifted around the space.

That was the George family way. Perception was more important than reality.

"I didn't intend to make a scene, Mother. But I'm sick and tired of you two looking down on anyone who isn't a blue-blooded trust fund baby." Riley shifted her gaze from her mother to her father, who'd leaned back in his seat and folded his arms over his chest.

"Well, I'm sorry if you think wanting what's best for my only daughter makes me a terrible father."

"I didn't say you're a terrible father." Riley rubbed her throbbing temple. "But it's presumptuous of you to assume you know what's best for me at this stage in my life. I'm not a child, Dad."

"But you are *my* child." Her father reached across the table and squeezed her hand. "You will always be my baby girl, Riley. I'll never stop worrying about you and wanting you to have everything you deserve in life."

"Everything *except* my inheritance. Because apparently, as the only female heir, I couldn't possibly be trusted to handle my own financial affairs." Riley stared knowingly at her father, tugging her hand from his.

Regardless of his feigned ignorance, she firmly believed he'd had a hand in the strange clause in her grandfather's will that singled her out.

"I'm going to the restroom." Her father stood abruptly and left the table. It was his way of signaling that the conversation was over.

Riley's mother folded her hands on the table and

smiled sweetly, employing her bona fide Southern belle tone of voice. "I know it isn't fair, honey. But you *will* get your inheritance just as soon as you've fulfilled the parameters of your grandfather's will."

"I shouldn't have to fulfill any sexist *additional* parameters," Riley noted. "It was just Grandad and Dad's way of trying to control me. But this is *my* life, not theirs. So if I choose to see Travis, that's my business."

"I realize he's handsome and charismatic. A celebrity. Dating a man like that is exciting. Believe me, I've had a few Travises in my past," her mother whispered conspiratorially. "But sweetheart, that isn't the kind of man you settle down with. You're so kind and nurturing. I know you're looking forward to becoming a wife and mother. But if you keep wasting your time with these eternal-bachelor types, you'll *never* get the husband and family you want."

Riley groaned quietly without reply. Because as much as she wanted to refute her mother's argument, she realized she wasn't completely wrong.

Eleven

Travis had taken the call from his agent because it must've been important for the woman to call him in the evening. But truthfully, he would've taken one of those spam calls trying to convince him his computer needed repair just to get away from that table.

Ted and Gina George were even more pretentious than he remembered. He honestly didn't know how someone as sweet and kind as Riley had come from that brood.

Is the money worth putting up with a year of dinner dates with Riley's parents?

If the money was strictly for him, his answer would be a resounding *hell no*. But he was doing this for his dad, for the legacy of Moonlight Ridge and for the employees who depended on it for their livelihood.

Travis went to the bar and ordered another boulevardier made with King's Finest bourbon. The bartender made his drink and Travis stuffed a five-dollar bill in the tip jar. He sipped his drink with a sense of relief.

"I'll have one of those," a familiar voice said.

Travis's spine stiffened. He sucked in a deep breath and turned to the man beside him. "I thought Cognac was your drink of choice, Mr. George."

"Good memory." Ted grinned. "But I find that trying another man's preferred drink offers insight into who he is."

"Is that right?" Travis eyed the older man who'd always reminded him of actor Laurence Fishburne. More so now that he'd gone all gray and put on a few pounds. "I'd love to hear what you come up with, but I should get back to the table. Riley will wonder where I've gone."

"Travis, can I be completely honest with you?" Ted asked before he could walk away.

"You mean you haven't been?" Travis raised an eyebrow. "Because you've been pretty clear that you don't think I'm good enough for your daughter."

"I know you must think Gina and I are some uppity Black folks who've forgotten who we are and where we come from. That we think we're better than you," Ted said. "Hell, I'd probably feel the same way if our roles were reversed. But son, I haven't forgotten where my family came from. I realize how fragile wealth and power can be. Like every other parent in the world, I want my children to have an even better life than I had. And out of all of my children, Riley is the one I have the highest hopes for. She's got a brilliant mind and a compassionate heart. I know she's going to do important things in her life—as long as she doesn't get thrown off track."

Travis finished his boulevardier and set the empty glass on the bar. "And you believe I'm going to derail your daughter from her destiny? Or rather, what you believe to be her destiny."

Ted took a healthy sip of the drink, then studied the glass. "Not bad."

"The boulevardier—that's what that drink is called, by the way—or my observation of why you think I'm not good enough for your daughter?"

"Both." Ted set the glass down. "Don't get me wrong, son, I'm not implying you're a bad person, and I don't believe you would intentionally harm my daughter. But when you live a certain kind of a life…things happen. Like that horrible accident you and your brothers were in. What if my daughter had been in that truck? She could've been seriously hurt. Maybe worse."

A knot tightened in Travis's gut. He'd gone to that restaurant to get an explanation from Riley, hoping she'd return to Moonlight Ridge with him. What if she had?

It had taken him more than a decade to admit that he needed to talk to a professional about the pent-up anger he had regarding the accident. To finally forgive himself for his immaturity that night that had put nearly everyone he'd loved in jeopardy. For him to stop laying blame at the feet of Riley and his brothers. But if something had happened to her or to Mack and Grey, he would never have forgiven himself.

"That was a long time ago, Mr. George," Travis said finally. "I'm not that hotheaded kid anymore. Believe me, if I was, our conversation earlier would've gone differently. I held my tongue because while it might've made me feel better to tell you what I think of your opinion of me and where you can stick it, it would've hurt Riley. And that's not something I want to do."

The man frowned. "I appreciate that you've settled

down somewhat, but now, just as then, my daughter is in over her head with a man like you. I regret how I broke you two up back then. Threatening to destroy your family's livelihood and reputation... To be honest, I feel bad about that. But my reasons for doing so were—"

"Hold up. *You* broke us up?" Travis pointed an accusatory finger. "As in, it wasn't Riley's idea to break up with me? You put her up to it by threatening my family?"

Heat flooded Travis's face. His shoulders stiffened, and his hands clenched so tightly that his short nails stabbed his palms, threatening to break the skin.

"What kind of man would do something so awful to his teenage daughter?" Travis's voice trembled as he tried to maintain his cool. He wanted to punch this pretentious asshole and leave him sprawled out on his back. Maybe knock loose a few of those brilliant white teeth.

"I'm not proud of what I did, son." The man's skin flushed as Travis's elevated voice drew the attention of the bartender and a few other patrons. "But I did what I did in the best interest of my daughter, so I won't apologize for it. If that's what I had to do to save her from a life of..." Ted's words trailed off. He ran a hand over his thinning hair. "Well, I'd do it again."

"I honestly don't know how your daughter managed to become such a decent, compassionate human being when she was raised by a heartless, self-centered egomaniac."

"It's what you do to protect your family. If you wouldn't go to the same lengths to protect yours, it only proves you're not the man I want for my daughter." Ted calmly finished his drink.

"People like to believe you can play nice and still get everything you want in life. It's a load of hippie bullshit," the older man continued. "A word of advice. Shit rolls downhill, son. If you're not willing to take what you want in this world and do whatever you have to do to defend it, then you'll never climb to the top of the heap. And if you do manage to somehow rise to the top, you won't stay there for long."

"Thanks, but no thanks, for your unsolicited advice. If I have to forgo human decency to claw my way to the top, I'm happy to stay where I am."

Despite Travis's celebrity status and business success, Ted George's net worth made him look like a pauper. And regardless of what he'd achieved in his life, Mr. George obviously still saw him as that abandoned foster kid Jameson Holloway had taken in. Maybe he always would. That was Ted's problem, not his. He wouldn't waste a moment trying to convince him otherwise.

"Have a good night, Mr. George." Travis leaned in, lowering his voice so only Ted could hear him. "And by that we both know I really mean go fuck yourself."

Travis turned and stalked toward their table. Riley's hopeful smile quickly turned into a tense frown as he approached. He felt bad for being the reason she suddenly looked stressed.

He forced a smile as he addressed her mother.

"Mrs. George, it was a pleasure to see you again, but I'm afraid another matter requires my attention." He turned toward Riley. "Are you leaving with me, babe, or would you prefer to stay and enjoy dessert with your parents? If so, I can send a driver back for you."

"No, I'm ready to go home." Riley stood, her eyes studying his as she grabbed her purse.

"Home?" Gina's eyes widened. "You two are living *together*?"

"Yes," they both proclaimed without hesitation, their eyes meeting.

"That's why I brought Travis tonight." Riley turned to her mother. "To tell you things are moving quickly between us. We've already lost so much time together."

"It was good seeing you again, Mrs. George." Travis dropped three crisp hundred-dollar bills on the table. Enough to cover the entire bill and leave their server a generous tip. He didn't want anything from Ted George. Not even dinner.

He took Riley's hand and they made their way to the valet outside without a word. When the valet left to retrieve Travis's car, she turned to face him.

"My father must've really pissed you off if you were willing to tell my parents we're living together." She looked up at him, her big brown eyes dripping with apology. "I'm sorry for what he said at the table and for whatever he said to make you so—"

"You don't need to apologize for your dad, Rye." His heart still thudded in his chest and his shoulders were tense. "And I'd rather not talk about what your father said right now."

"Whatever you want. I'm just glad that after tonight you're still considering my offer."

"We'll talk more about that later, too." He still hadn't decided what he planned to do. "How about we talk about it back at *our* place, since we're apparently living together now?"

He still couldn't believe he'd stepped into that one. But he was so pissed at Ted and annoyed with Gina that it had given him a perverse sense of joy to tell him off and shock her.

"I said *home* inadvertently. But when my mother questioned it, I couldn't help turning the knife a little. It was immature, and I'm sorry I dragged you into it."

"I get it. My reasons for going along with it were pretty much the same." He shrugged.

"It wasn't exactly a lie," she said, glancing around them fondly. "Being here in Asheville… I feel more at home than I've felt in a long time. It's different from when we were kids, but I love the laid-back vibe and the amazing art scene. The historic architecture at places like the Basilica, Moonlight Ridge and the Biltmore." She gestured toward the grand estate in the distance. "I've found this incredible joy here."

"Were you unhappy before?" Travis studied her warm brown eyes.

"I never thought of myself as being *unhappy*." Riley shrugged. "I have a good life. I'm doing important work. I'm in good health. I don't have cause to complain."

"That isn't an answer." Travis lifted a hand to her cheek.

"No, it isn't." She gave him a sad smile. "I've been happier here the past few weeks than I've been in a while. How's that?"

"Fair enough." He could relate to that.

Travis helped Riley inside the car when it arrived. He tried not to notice how the hem of her dress rose a few inches as she slid into her seat, but he couldn't help himself. Nor could he help noting that his feelings toward her had changed considerably.

This is just a business deal.

Travis repeated the words in his head again and again. It was a reality he couldn't afford to forget. Otherwise he might be in serious danger of falling for the princess who'd once captured his heart.

Twelve

Riley padded around the cottage barefoot while Travis was upstairs taking another call from his agent. She couldn't believe he was staying in the same cottage they'd made out in a few times as teens. At the time, she hadn't been ready to take things further. Travis had been the perfect gentleman, never pressuring her for anything more.

Riley often regretted that Travis hadn't been her first instead of the impatient, subpar oaf she'd given her virginity to in college.

Travis trotted down the stairs, barefoot, tugging his shirt down over his rather impressive abs. The imprint in his gray sweatpants offered a hint of what lay beneath.

A quiet sigh escaped her mouth and she sank her teeth into her lower lip.

Travis's food isn't the only thing about him that's mouthwatering.

"Sorry to keep you waiting." He went straight for the little bar in the corner of the room. "With the rising popularity of the gastropub in London, my agent is pushing me to do a guest spot on a cooking network in the UK."

"Sounds like a great opportunity." Riley watched as Travis made a rum and Coke.

"It is." He handed it to her, then started making another. "But I have a lot going on right now with the show, the resort and the business. And apparently I've acquired a fiancée."

Riley was sipping her drink and wondering if he'd take the UK op when his words finally registered. She put down her glass. "Does that mean you accept my proposal?"

He climbed on one of the barstools and patted the other.

She sat beside him, as he'd silently requested. Something in his dark eyes gave her pause.

Travis studied his glass. "Why didn't you tell me what really happened that night?"

Riley's pulse quickened. Travis didn't need to specify which night. She thought of everything in her life as happening either before or after *that* night.

"My dad told you?" She could strangle her father. No wonder Travis couldn't wait to get out of there. Her father had the audacity to gloat about his role in the events of that night.

"That he threatened to destroy my family if you didn't walk away?" Travis gripped his glass so tightly she feared he'd shatter it. Riley placed a gentle hand on his forearm, and he loosened his grasp. He sucked in a deep breath, then sighed. "I knew your dad didn't want us to see each other, but I never imagined he'd do something so underhanded."

Behind the scenes, Ted George did whatever it took to get what he wanted. But he carefully cultivated his image as a generous family man who was a pillar of the community. So Riley was surprised he'd admitted to blackmailing his own daughter. He'd evidently wanted Travis to know he wasn't above stooping so low again.

"Said he felt bad about it in one breath, then told me he'd do it again in a heartbeat with the next." Travis gulped his rum and Coke.

The pain in his voice made Riley's heart ache. Her father was an asshole, and she planned to tell him as much—in person—in the morning.

"I'm sorry I couldn't tell you the truth then, and I'm sorry my father was so horrible to you…then and now. I wouldn't blame you for hating my family. Nor would I blame you for deciding you don't want to do this."

He looked at her, his head cocked as if seeing her clearly for the first time. Travis tugged Riley off her stool so that she stood between his widened legs. His eyes met hers.

"I should've known that note you wrote and the way you reacted at the restaurant… That wasn't the girl I'd fallen in love with." He cupped her cheek and offered a pained smile. "I'm sorry I believed the worst of you."

"Don't be." Tears stung her eyes as she recalled the horrible choice she'd been forced to make. What had hurt most was knowing she'd hurt him and he'd hate her for it. That all of the beautiful memories they'd created would be destroyed. "That's exactly what my father wanted you to believe. He wanted you to be hurt, and he wanted me to be the one to do it. He knew if I wounded your pride you wouldn't want anything else to do with me."

"I spent so many years blaming you for what happened," he said finally. "But the truth is it was all my fault."

"It was an accident, Travis. It could've happened to any one of us. We've spent enough time blaming ourselves. Time that would've been better spent helping each other recover. Physically, mentally, emotionally." The tears that burned her eyes spilled down her cheeks. Her face was hot with embarrassment. "I know your world was turned upside down that night, Travis. But so was mine."

He handed her a cocktail napkin and she dabbed her tears.

"Why was that night so devastating for you?" His expression was pained and his question sincere. "You got to go on with your life as if nothing had ever happened. You moved on."

"I didn't just move on," she protested, fresh tears welling in her eyes.

What right did the poor little rich girl whose asshole father had precipitated the entire mess have to shed tears over what she'd lost that night?

Yet, she'd been devastated.

Every rejection by Travis after the crash sank her deeper into depression. When she'd overheard her parents discussing whether they should send her away to a hospital facility, fearing she might harm herself, she'd realized how deeply she'd sunk into the abyss. She'd finally admitted that she'd needed to see a mental health professional. It was her only hope of climbing out of the dark hole she'd fallen into. But there was no need to burden him with any of that.

"I couldn't bear that our last conversation was me telling you I didn't want you in my life anymore." She dabbed the rapidly falling tears. "Nothing could've been further from the truth."

Travis stood, wrapping her in his strong arms. He held her, her tears wetting his shirt.

Riley felt foolish making a spectacle of herself. But she couldn't ever remember feeling safer than she felt in Travis's arms now.

He let her cry, his large hand rubbing slow circles on her back. Finally, he said, "So about this proposal of yours. I'll do it. But that additional 100K won't be a gift. Let's establish it as a line of credit. I'm not looking to take advantage of you here, Riley. This deal should be mutually beneficial to all parties."

Riley was stunned by his insistence on repaying the bonus. It was more than fair in light of the long-term commitment required. He was a busy celebrity, and his time was valuable. She realized that. Besides, that money was a small percentage of her sizable inheritance.

"Thank you, Travis. But you don't need to—"

"I know, and I appreciate it." Travis shoved his hands in his pockets, which inadvertently highlighted the impressive imprint in those otherwise innocuous gray sweatpants.

A chill ran down her spine and her nipples beaded in response.

"So how do we do this?" he asked.

Wow. Travis had actually agreed to her marriage-of-convenience scheme. She'd worked so hard to get to this point that she hadn't given much thought to what happened next.

"We...get engaged?" It was more of a question than a plan.

"Okay. When do we announce it?"

"My focus needs to be on the gala for the next few weeks. But soon after?"

"All right." Travis moved behind the bar and refreshed their drinks. "And since you told your mother we're living together, I assume you'll be moving in here right away."

Riley couldn't believe she'd said that to her mother or that Travis had been gracious enough to play along.

"I understand if you're not ready for that yet," she said. "Maybe I could rent a nearby cottage. We could just say I'm living here." She accepted the refreshed drink from Travis.

"My father would find out. We need to convince him this relationship is real, too," he reminded her. "So you'll need to move in here."

Travis stated it without emotion, as a simple fact.

"When you check out on Sunday, bring your bags here. As for sleeping arrangements... Only the master bedroom has a bed in it. The second bedroom only has a desk. You take the bed. I'll sleep on the couch until I can get another bed for the guest room."

Riley should be grateful for his gentlemanly offer. Instead, she was disappointed and couldn't help noticing the way his shirt clung to his well-developed chest. Nor could she help eyeing the dickprint in his sweatpants.

God, she was awful.

"I won't put you out of your own bed, Travis. Why can't we just share it?"

He assessed her wearily. "You're sure about this?"

"It's a California king-size bed," she said. "We could both spread out like starfish and barely touch...if we didn't want to."

But I definitely want to.

She gulped some of her drink, hoping to drown out the too-honest voice in her head.

"All right," Travis agreed. "And I have a double master at my place in Atlanta."

"Then we'll only have to share a bed for a few months. And only when we're both in town at the same time." She forced a smile. "I'll have to make trips to Charlotte, plus I have a couple of business conferences scheduled soon. And you'll probably have to travel to LA and to some of your restaurants. This is going to be perfect. Thank you, Travis."

She bounced on her heels, excited that everything was falling into place.

His attention was drawn to her breasts, and his eyes drifted shut momentarily before he met her gaze again. Then they fleshed out their plan.

Travis would talk to Autumn and reserve a date so they could get married at Moonlight Ridge. And he noted that since it wasn't a real marriage, she should let Autumn plan everything so she could focus on her philanthropic efforts.

Riley realized this wouldn't be a *real* marriage. Still, it smarted when Travis said it.

She set her drink on the bar. "I have an early start tomorrow. You probably do, too. I'd better head back to my room."

"Or you could just stay here." Travis shrugged. "I can loan you a T-shirt to sleep in."

She nodded, her heart beating faster. "Sure. Thanks."

Then they both picked up their glasses and drained them.

Maybe she wasn't the only one who was nervous about sharing a bed.

Thirteen

It's a California king-size bed. We could both spread out like starfish and barely touch if we didn't want to.

The words replayed in Travis's head as his feet pounded the mulch that padded the scenic trail around the lake.

Perhaps their conscious minds realized that this would be far less complicated if they kept their hands to themselves. But their subconscious minds maintained a different opinion.

They'd gone to sleep, each of them clinging to their respective corners of the bed. But at some point, they'd both drifted toward the center. He awoke to Riley's soft, warm body nestled against his. She'd thrown one arm across his stomach and her leg over his. Her head rested against his shoulder as she slept soundly.

He hadn't wanted to wake her, so he hadn't attempted

to uncoil her limbs from his. Later, he'd awakened to find himself holding her in his arms, his chin resting atop her head. As if they were a couple accustomed to sharing a bed.

Holding Riley in his arms as she slept was comforting. But it had also alarmed him. They'd sorted out their past, but neither of them had indicated any interest in exploring a future together. There were too many years and too many painful memories to wade through.

Besides, hadn't Riley presented him with this fake-marriage proposal because she wasn't interested in doing this with someone who'd mistake it for an actual relationship?

She wasn't interested in a romantic entanglement, and neither was he. They were both focused on their work. Anything else was an unwelcome distraction.

Snuggling—consciously or not—wasn't a good move. Waking up with a raging hard-on and thoughts of how amazing she'd looked in that body-hugging dress and those sexy high heels? That was a terrible, horrible, no-good, extremely insane idea.

He'd awakened at a little after 5:30 a.m. and managed to slide from beneath Riley without waking her. Then he'd gone downstairs and done push-ups and sit-ups until his chest and abs burned. Once it was light enough, he hit the trail around the lake a few times.

But it was getting late. He needed to return to the cottage, shower and get over to the main kitchen. This afternoon, they were serving their fabulous new menu to the staff—including Jameson, Giada, Mack, Molly, Grey and Autumn.

The tasting menu consisted of bananas foster French toast; espresso waffles with hazelnut drizzle; red vel-

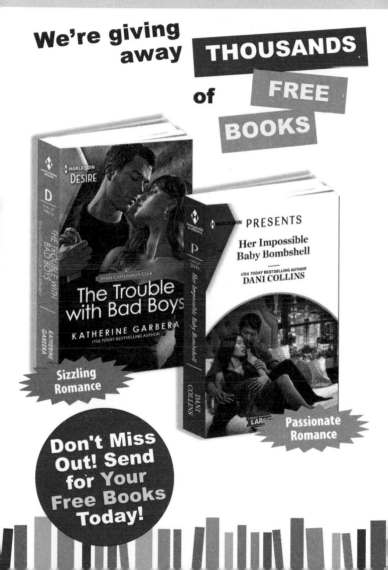

Get up to 4
FREE FABULOUS BOOKS
You Love!

To thank you for being a loyal reader we'd like to send you up to 4 FREE BOOKS, absolutely free.

Just write "YES" on the Loyal Reader Voucher and we'll send you up to 4 Free Books and Free Mystery Gifts, altogether worth over $20, as a way of saying thank you for being a loyal reader.

Try **Harlequin® Desire** books featuring the worlds of the American elite with juicy plot twists, delicious sensuality and intriguing scandal.

Try **Harlequin Presents®** Larger-print books featuring the glamourous lives of royals and billionaires in a world of exotic locations, where passion knows no bounds.

Or **TRY BOTH!**

We are so glad you love the books as much as we do and can't wait to send you great new books.

So don't miss out, return your Loyal Reader Voucher Today!

Pam Powers

LOYAL READER
FREE BOOKS VOUCHER

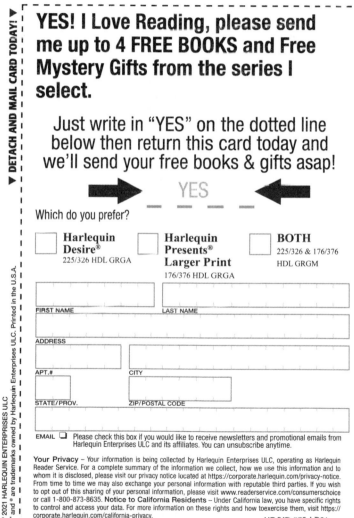

◄ DETACH AND MAIL CARD TODAY! ▼

YES! I Love Reading, please send me up to 4 FREE BOOKS and Free Mystery Gifts from the series I select.

Just write in "YES" on the dotted line below then return this card today and we'll send your free books & gifts asap!

➡ YES ⬅ - - - -

Which do you prefer?

☐ **Harlequin Desire®**
225/326 HDL GRGA

☐ **Harlequin Presents® Larger Print**
176/376 HDL GRGA

☐ **BOTH**
225/326 & 176/376 HDL GRGM

FIRST NAME

LAST NAME

ADDRESS

APT.#

CITY

STATE/PROV.

ZIP/POSTAL CODE

EMAIL ☐ Please check this box if you would like to receive newsletters and promotional emails from Harlequin Enterprises ULC and its affiliates. You can unsubscribe anytime.

HD/HP-520-LR21

vet pancakes; blackberry lemon ricotta scones; Gruyère, Parmesan and chives soufflé; quiche Lorraine with delicious brown sugar caramelized bacon; and eggs Benedict. Each was a complete treat for the senses meant to ensure Moonlight Ridge would become a bona fide brunch destination. And on the brunch drink menu: peach Bellinis, kir royale and mimosas.

Still, he was nervous. Each restaurant he opened was more than just a business. It was a manifestation of himself. Part of a legacy he was building. But the menu they were rolling out for Moonlight Ridge felt even more personal. He wanted the resort to thrive again because nothing would make his father happier. And as kind and generous as Jameson Holloway had been to everyone in his life, he deserved that kind of happiness.

Travis jogged back to the cottage, cooled down and stretched before stepping inside.

"Hey." Riley emerged from the kitchen in her own T-shirt and another pair of body-hugging leggings. "How was your run?"

"Great." He inhaled the scent of his preferred brand of Jamaican coffee. "You made coffee?"

"I did," she confirmed. "And I had my things brought over so I could shower and change. I hope you don't mind." She seemed to hold her breath in anticipation of his reaction.

"No, it's fine," Travis said. "I'm gonna hop into the shower first."

Travis jogged upstairs, got out of his sweaty clothing and climbed into the shower, trying not to think of how incredible Riley looked in those leggings.

He hadn't gone to the shower with the intention of relieving the tension that had been building low in his belly since he'd awakened to Riley's warm body all over his. Her hair was spread across the pillow and shielded her gorgeous face. And she'd looked unbelievably sexy wearing his Carolina Panthers T-shirt. Then, in the kitchen, those leggings showcased every morsel of that curvy ass.

Could he really be blamed for a little hand action?

He'd taken his painfully hard dick in one soapy hand, the other pressed against the wall. His fist glided up and down the slick skin, slowly at first. Then faster, as Technicolor-vivid visions of Riley filtered through his brain. Until he'd finally reached his pinnacle, shooting hot, sticky fluid against the shower wall.

Travis slumped against the cold tile of the back wall, his body spent, his heart racing as he caught his breath. If he and Riley George were going to live together platonically, it seemed his right hand was going to become his new best friend.

Riley rearranged the flowers she'd placed in a vase.

"Those are beautiful, Rye. What's the occasion?"

"My way of saying thank you." Riley grabbed a mug. "Coffee?"

"Please. Black with sugar." Travis sat at the table. "And you don't need to thank me."

"I do," she insisted. "You're going along with this whole thing. You didn't deck my father last night, though I'm sure you wanted to." She handed him his coffee. "And you're letting me move in here sooner than you'd hoped. Flowers don't even begin to express my gratitude."

"But helping us renovate this place does, so thank you."

They drank their coffee in relative silence, a million thoughts running through her head.

"Having second thoughts about the marriage?" Travis watched her carefully.

"No, I was just thinking…" Riley shrugged. "It's silly."

"I won't laugh." He raised a hand. "Promise."

Riley sighed. "I used to doodle our names in the back of my notebooks."

One corner of his mouth lifted. "Like 'Travis loves Riley'?"

They'd carved those very words in a tree in the woods. Was it still out there?

"More like Riley Anne George-Holloway," she said. "And you promised not to laugh."

"I'm not. It's adorable." His mouth pulled into a lopsided grin. "Must seem surreal that it's actually going to happen."

"Yes, but it's also kind of…sad, I guess. We were head over heels in love back then. I would never have imagined us getting married as part of some business agreement." She sipped her coffee.

"You'll get your fantasy wedding one day, Rye." Travis squeezed her hand.

"Maybe." Riley shrugged.

Their wedding would be simple and elegant. Efficient. She wouldn't waste a ton of time and resources on something that wasn't real. Still, not getting her dream wedding was monumentally disappointing. She hadn't expected that.

"You sure you're okay?" Travis took his coffee mug to the sink.

"Yes, of course." Riley forced a smile. "Like I said, it was silly."

Travis confirmed she'd be joining them for the tasting of the new Moonlight Ridge brunch menu at noon.

Then he handed her a slip of paper with the key code to the cottage.

Riley thanked him again and lifted onto her toes and kissed his cheek.

Travis looked down at her, his dark eyes indecipherable. "See you at noon."

"Do *not* fall for Travis Holloway," she whispered under her breath as she watched him leave. But as her heart swelled and a cascade of emotions swirled around her, it was clear her heart and body weren't listening.

Fourteen

Riley surveyed Moonlight Ridge's grand ballroom. In a few hours, the room would be filled to capacity. They'd sold out the larger venue in record time—thanks to celebrity chef Travis Holloway being the main attraction—and the resort was completely booked. Molly, Ross, Milo and their teams had exceeded her expectations for the *Great Gatsby*–themed event. The decor was stunning.

Thanks to her assistant, Adele, members of the charity's staff, a team of volunteers and the resort employees, nearly everything was set for the event.

Riley reviewed the printed program to ensure she hadn't missed anything.

"You've been going like the Energizer Bunny since before the sun came up." Travis approached her, his expression filled with concern. "Have you eaten?"

"Not yet." Riley rearranged a place setting. "I need to make sure everything is perfect."

"Rye, take a breath. Everything is under control. You can spare a moment to eat."

His no-nonsense expression indicated he wasn't taking no for an answer.

Riley's stomach rumbled and she felt a bit faint. "Okay. But I have to get ready soon."

"I've got you." Travis's low, deep voice flowed over her like warm honey and sent a shiver down her spine.

Travis *had* been there for her these past few weeks.

He'd helped her with the preparations for the gala well beyond his obligations as the headline chef. His PR team had secured coverage on local and national news and talk shows. And Travis had appeared on many of those shows himself, despite his crazy schedule.

They shared a living space and frequently worked side by side after hours on the sofa or at the kitchen table. So Riley had seen firsthand how busy Travis was. But after sharing a bed those first few weeks, he'd ordered a bed for the guest room, and she'd been relegated there.

Riley missed their late nights together in bed, silently tapping away on their laptops. But at least they shared breakfast most days and dinner most nights. They even spent some evenings watching a movie together or playing the occasional board game. It was…*nice*. Very different from her solitary life in her pricey town house in Uptown Charlotte.

Her favorite day was Sunday, when Jameson gathered his sons and their significant others around his dining table over a delicious meal prepared by Giada or Travis. Riley loved the friendship she was building with Travis's family. She adored Molly and she was enjoying getting to know Autumn. Grey was sweet and easy to get along with. Funny. Mack had been a tough nut to crack, but he'd softened.

Then there was Travis.

They'd been rebuilding their friendship little by little, even as they presented themselves to the world as a couple. Yet, every time he held her hand or kissed her for the benefit of his family or hers, it felt a little less like a show and a lot more real. Because she genuinely felt the emotions they were putting on display: admiration, affection, desire.

Did Travis feel the same?

He'd given zero indication he felt anything more for her. So maybe that was her answer. But at least he'd signed the agreement and committed to marrying her sometime after the gala.

"Come with me." Travis guided her to a table in the corner of the room. He lifted the stainless-steel dome with a flourish, revealing his signature chicken salad—with walnuts, cranberries and thinly sliced grapes—served on a warm, freshly made croissant.

Her favorite.

She thanked him and cleaned her hands with a moist towelette. Then she took the first satisfying bite of her sandwich. The combination of savory flavors melded on her palate.

"So good," she muttered through a mouthful.

"I have to get back to the kitchen. I want tonight to be perfect, too." He winked at her, and she felt more at ease than she had all morning.

"Travis." Hallie jogged toward them with members of the reality show filming crew right behind her. "We've got a problem."

"What's wrong?"

"The filet mignon is gone," she huffed.

"What do you mean *gone*?" Despite Travis's calm facade, his voice was tense.

"What do you mean the filet mignon is gone?" Riley repeated, suddenly feeling nauseous. Donors had paid ten thousand dollars per table to be here tonight. And they'd preselected their meals.

Offering substitutions wasn't an option.

"Not all of it is gone," Hallie said. "But there isn't enough to meet the orders for the gala tonight. I don't know how this happened, I swear."

"And you're sure you didn't overlook it?" Travis walked briskly toward the elevator that led down to the kitchen. Hallie and Riley were both hot on his heels.

"Maybe the delivery was short, and we just didn't notice," Riley offered.

"I took inventory myself," Travis said. "It was there, and it sure as hell didn't grow legs and walk out of here on its own, so let's find it."

Riley joined Travis and Hallie on the elevator, her heart thumping. Her stomach dropped to her knees and her head spun. A blunder like this would leave their high-profile donors seething, regardless of how hot and charming their star chef was. She was grateful when Travis insisted the film crew take the stairs.

"We'll have to cancel the event tonight, won't we?" Riley asked. This was going to be a PR debacle.

"Babe, listen to me." Travis cradled her cheek. His voice was calm. "Everything will be fine. I'll do whatever I need to do to make this right. I promise."

The elevator door slid open and Hallie exited. Travis

hit the button to close the door again. He turned to Riley and held on to her waist, her back pressed against the wall.

"I know this looks bad, Rye, but I've dealt with a lot worse and still managed to pull off the event without anyone noticing." Travis dropped a soft kiss to her cheek and another on her lips. For the briefest moment, Riley forgot that her world was crumbling around her.

Her father had vehemently objected to moving the event to Moonlight Ridge and having Travis headline it. So if tonight's event crashed and burned, she'd never hear the end of it.

"If I'm not panicking, you shouldn't, either. Go on and get all glammed up, beautiful. I've got this." His mouth curved in a soft grin.

Riley nodded, feeling numb as she watched him exit the elevator into the kitchen. She hit the button and watched the doors close, praying everything would be okay.

Fifteen

Travis joined Hallie in the walk-in refrigerator where there was considerably less filet mignon than there had been the day before. A knot tightened in his gut.

"I'm going to get fired, aren't I?" Hallie clutched her stomach, then answered her own question. "I'm *definitely* going to get fired."

"Relax, Hal. You're good. I know you didn't do this," Travis said calmly. "But someone certainly did. Ask Ross and every single person in this kitchen if they know anything about this. Meanwhile, I'm going to recheck every square inch of this fridge."

He'd rip the place apart if he needed to. If those premium cuts of meat were still in that fridge, he'd find them. Travis started a systematic search. Once Hallie finished questioning all of the staff about the missing meat, she returned and helped him look.

The meat wasn't there.

He enlisted Hallie and dishwashers Pauly and Ernesto to help them search the freezer.

Travis was on the verge of having his assistant call every reputable meat vendor in town—when he shifted a stack of frozen butter. The missing cuts of meat were there, frozen. This was no mistake. The filet mignon had been placed there intentionally.

"Who the hell would put them in here behind the butter?" Hallie asked.

"Someone who didn't want us to find them," Travis replied.

"Who'd do that?" Hallie rubbed her arms to warm them. "Everyone here understands how important this event is to Moonlight Ridge."

"Maybe that was the point," Travis mused. "To sabotage tonight's event."

"Could the film crew have done this? Maybe they were trying to manufacture some drama for the show," Hallie whispered to Travis so the film crew couldn't hear her.

"They wouldn't have done this. But we'll worry about who did later," Travis said. "Right now, let's get this meat defrosted."

Thankfully, there was more than enough time to defrost the meat and get it prepped for dinner. But he needed to talk to Mack and Grey. Their elusive thief was likely behind this. If he hadn't found the thief's cache, he'd bet that filet mignon would've made its way onto the black market where disreputable restaurants and hotels sourced their goods.

A forensic accountant had combed over the books, and Mack and Grey had locked down Moonlight Ridge's expenditures, making it more difficult for theft to go undetected. Selling meat and other high-value goods on the black market was likely the thief's only option.

But for now, crisis averted.

He dialed Riley. "Hey, Rye. There was just a little mix-up. We're good to go."

"Thank you, Travis." She sounded relieved. "But I just stepped out of the shower, so I need to get dressed."

He was speaking to Riley *naked*? Travis shut his eyes against that visual. Something he found himself doing whenever he heard her shower running at the cottage because that vivid image had practically given him a hard-on.

"Should've placed a video call," he muttered, and she giggled.

They were flirting. Not as a pretense, but because he was wildly attracted to her and they genuinely enjoyed spending time together. So against his better judgment, they'd been teasing and flirting. A lot.

It was harmless, as long as they didn't cross the line. And he'd gotten dangerously close to doing just that.

"Sorry, I shouldn't have said that." Travis walked into the kitchen office and shut the door. He turned on the speakerphone and rummaged through a file containing meat purchase orders. "Got a little carried away at the thought of you…well, you know."

"You're the one who put me out of your bed," she reminded him. "Tonight, you're going to regret that." The flirtatious lilt of Riley's voice made his pulse quicken. Electricity traveled the length of his spine.

"What's that supposed to mean?"

"That if we were sharing a bed, maybe I'd find a special way to thank you for saving the day."

His mouth fell open, but he was speechless as all the possibilities ran through his head.

When he didn't respond, Riley laughed. "Bye, Travis."

His heart thumped. For the past few weeks, he'd done his level best to ignore the way his body reacted to hers as she traipsed around the cottage in tiny sleep shorts and a midriff-baring top. But there was something particularly attractive about her moving about the cottage in his borrowed, oversize T-shirts.

It was ridiculous, and maybe even a little sexist... But he liked the idea of her body being draped in something that belonged to him. As if—by extension—it did, too.

"You kicked her out of your bed?" Grey stood in the doorway with his arms folded. "Seriously?"

"Still eavesdropping, I see. Is there something that actually is your business I can help you with?" Travis returned to digging through the files.

Grey fell into the chair beside the desk. "Autumn and Molly saw the three of you leaving the ballroom like you were in Jurassic Park and the dinosaurs got loose. They sent me down here to make sure everything is okay."

"Everything is fine. Now," Travis added.

"What happened?" Grey sat up straight in the chair.

Travis explained what had happened and shared his suspicions about the thief being a saboteur determined to see the place go down in flames.

"It must be someone in the kitchen." Grey rubbed his chin. "That narrows down the suspects. Maybe you were right about Hallie. We know she needs the money. When Pops met her, she was stealing meat from a grocery store. Maybe she's doing it again."

"She was a teenager shoplifting a ham and canned vegetables to feed her aged grandmother and younger siblings on Christmas," Travis pointed out. "I've been there. But I've gotten to know her, and I honestly don't believe she'd do anything to hurt Pops. She loves him like a father, and she feels like she owes him. He changed her life."

"Then do you have any theories on who it might be?"

"Nothing I can substantiate yet. But I am sure about who it *isn't*. And Hallie's at the top of that list." Travis pulled out the file folder, then slid into the chair. He shoved the file of meat purchase invoices toward his brother. "I'd start with these. Check to see if there have been other missing inventory items that caused Dad or the resort any kind of embarrassment."

"I'm on it." Grey flipped through the file. "Now, why on earth would you kick Riley out of your bed? I thought things were good between you two. And you're obviously still into her."

"Things are good between us, and I'd like to keep them that way. So I'm not trying to fuck with her head or mine."

"If you have feelings for her and she evidently has feelings for you—"

"I have no idea what this is, where it's going or if I even want it." His voice was tinged with frustration over his constantly evolving feelings for Riley. "Yes, I was in love with her then. And yes, I like and respect her now. But our lives are on different trajectories. At some point, she'll need to return to Charlotte, and I need to return to Atlanta and then LA. If we move forward with plans for a Traverser restaurant in New York, I'll probably get a place there. What then?"

Grey shrugged. "Guess that depends on what you both want and how badly you want it."

His brother had gone to school and worked in New York, and he still had a green-building architecture firm based there. But like Mack, Grey had fallen in love with a woman who seemed to be his perfect match and with Moonlight Ridge again. Neither of his brothers had returned to their old lives.

Travis loved his family and this old place, but he had no intention of staying here.

He had a life to get back to, and so did Riley. There'd be no happy ending for them, and a meaningless fling for the next year felt like a monumentally bad idea. He was already in his feelings about her, so the stakes were just too high, and he didn't see that changing. It was better not to start something that would only hurt both of them.

"Now, I have much bigger issues to handle. I have a ballroom full of folks coming for this gala tonight, and someone has gone to great lengths to sabotage it. I doubt they'll stop there."

Grey stood. "I'll update Mack on what happened. We'll both be on the lookout. Call us if you need anything."

"Thanks, G." Travis bumped Grey's offered fist. "I'll keep that in mind."

"You'd better." Grey closed the door behind him.

He'd become accustomed to taking on everything himself, afraid of being let down. But it felt good to know he had his brothers there to back him up, and he'd missed that.

The Holloway brothers against the world.

Travis would make sure this event went off without a hitch. For Jameson. For Moonlight Ridge. And for Riley.

He opened the bottom desk drawer and looked at the item he'd hidden there earlier.

Yes, he had much bigger things to worry about tonight indeed.

Sixteen

It was nearly the end of the night and Riley was exhausted, but incredibly proud. The gala had gone flawlessly. The room was packed, and the guests were raving over their meals—especially the filet mignon.

The decorations were splendid. It felt like they'd been transported back to the Jazz Age. And everyone in attendance had really embraced the theme.

Most of the men wore suits that looked like something Leonardo DiCaprio would've worn in *The Great Gatsby*. Many had donned felt fedoras or classic homburg hats. Nearly all of them wore lapel collar vests that matched their suits and had the requisite pocket watch on a chain. And the two-tone oxfords were definitely a hit.

The ladies in attendance looked wonderful. There were lots of sparkling sequins and beaded dresses with flapper fringe, much like the jewel-green vintage dropped-waist dress she wore. Black fringe hung from the scalloped hem at her knees down to her ankles. She'd accessorized the dress with a black beaded headband with black feathers, and black fingerless gloves. T-strap pumps completed the outfit.

The live band had played classic jazz by all the greats: Duke Ellington, Miles Davis, Benny Goodman, Dizzy Gillespie, Ella Fitzgerald, Dave Brubeck and more. But they were currently playing "Sugar" by Maroon 5 and the dance floor was full.

"I have to give it to you, sweetheart. You've pulled off quite a feat," her father said as he and her mother approached, both of them smiling. "It seems Moonlight Ridge was the perfect choice."

"And we all love Chef Henri, but he couldn't have pulled the crowd and sponsorships Travis did. I hear you had a few hundred people wait-listed," her mother gushed.

"Thank you." Riley hated that she still wanted her parents' approval, despite their sharply different life philosophies. "It's big of you to admit you were wrong about this place and Travis."

"That's *not* what I said, Princess," her father objected. "And what your mother meant is it was a good *business* decision to replace Henri with the Holloway boy."

"He's no more a boy than you are, Dad." Riley folded her arms.

"You aren't actually comparing me to that—"

"Travis, dear, hello," her mother said loudly.

Riley and her father turned toward Travis. He'd changed out of the white chef's jacket and looked good enough to eat.

She sank her teeth into her lower lip as she scanned

this incredibly sexy man. The white dinner jacket set off his dark brown skin. She envisioned taking Travis back to the cottage and stripping him out of the jacket and those slim black tuxedo pants. Totally inappropriate since they were fake-dating and she was standing with her parents, who noticed her reaction.

Of the four of them, only Travis seemed oblivious about how much she wanted him.

"Good evening, Mr. and Mrs. George." Travis addressed her parents, but his gaze was on her. "Hey there, Princess."

Her father huffed when Travis used his pet name for her.

"You clean up nice." She grinned. "The black-and-white combo looks good on you."

"And you look stunning." His eyes roamed down her body before returning to her heated face. "You put on one hell of an event, Rye. You should be proud of yourself."

"I am." Her breathing became shallow when he leaned down and kissed her temple.

"I'm proud of you, too." He whispered the words meant only for her.

Her heart felt full and her eyes were misty. Why had Travis's sincere praise moved her to tears? Because he and his brothers were the reason she supported this charity. Many older children in the foster system didn't find forever homes as Travis, Mack and Grey had.

"Dance with me?" Travis extended his palm.

She hadn't danced all night, but she couldn't resist Travis's soft plea or the entrancing way he stared at her as if it was only the two of them in the room. She slid her hand into his.

"Excuse us," Travis said to her parents, whom she'd

momentarily forgotten about. He led her onto the parquet dance floor in front of the stage.

The song ended, but no other song followed.

"Why'd they stop playing?" Riley glanced at the stage. "Everyone is sitting down."

"Maybe there's a good reason." Travis grinned.

"What reason could they possibly have for—"

"Thank you to each and every one of you for being here tonight and your generous contributions." The executive director of the charity took the stage. "Please give a special thank-you to the George Family Foundation and to Ms. Riley George for her tireless efforts tonight."

Suddenly, there was a spotlight on her. Her heart swelled as everyone stood and clapped. Riley nodded her thanks to the executive director and the applauding crowd.

"You knew about this?" She smiled at Travis, whose grin deepened. He joined the applause. His dark eyes were filled with affection. She blinked back tears.

Next, the executive director requested a round of applause for Chef Travis Holloway. The spotlight moved to him as she showed an enlarged version of the huge check Travis had written to the charity—it represented a sizable chunk of his appearance fee.

The woman had one more announcement.

"You may not know this, but Travis and Riley have a long history. They met right here, on the grounds of this hotel, as children."

The spotlight had moved onto both of them as the woman shared how they'd dated as teens and reconnected after he'd stepped in for Chef Henri.

Riley's face flushed and she was pretty sure the room was spinning.

She whispered to Travis, "What is happening right now?"

He squeezed her hand. "Wait and see."

"Travis would like to dedicate a special song to Riley. Travis and Riley, the floor is yours." The woman gestured toward the empty dance floor.

It was sweet. Also, totally embarrassing. Her cheeks burned, and the giant spotlight wasn't helping.

They walked to the middle of the floor and Travis slid an arm around her waist as the band started to play the opening chords of "A Fool for You." The lead singer belted out the lyrics about a deep, enduring, unconditional love.

She hadn't heard the song in years until it came on the radio a few weeks ago. She'd played it often in her room since then. Travis had evidently noticed.

Riley glanced over at her parents. Her father glared at them. Her mother regarded them with what felt like a mixture of envy and alarm.

She'd worry about her parents later. Right now, she would focus on Travis's thoughtful gesture. But before the song ended, Travis went down on one knee and pulled a black velvet box from inside his jacket.

He wasn't going to… *Oh my God. Yes, he is.*

"Riley, I fell in love with you when we were just teenagers. And after all this time, it feels like nothing between us has changed. We've wasted so much of our lives apart. I don't want to waste another second. Marry me, Rye. Please."

She stared at him, one hand covering her mouth. This was all an act for their parents and the TV crew. She realized that. But he'd given her the grand gesture she'd bemoaned missing out on. And everything he'd said and all of the emotions running through her head felt incredibly real.

Riley lowered her hand and held it out to him as tears slid down her face.

"Yes, Travis." She nodded. "Baby, I can't wait to marry you."

Travis slid the gorgeous diamond solitaire onto her finger and stood. He kissed her as the room exploded with thunderous applause. When Travis finally released her, they turned and waved to the crowd cheering them on. The cameras were rolling, but her parents were no longer there.

It wasn't a surprise, but that didn't stop it from hurting. Riley glanced to the other side of the room where Travis's family was seated. Everyone at the table was clapping. Giada and Molly wiped away tears. Even Mack and Grey, who were aware of their deal, seemed moved.

The table where her family had been seated was empty, and her heart felt empty, too.

"They'll come around, sweetheart. Until then, I've got enough family for both of us." Travis indicated his family smiling and applauding.

Riley blew them a kiss, her eyes filled with tears. For the next year the Holloways would be her family, too. Just the thought of spending Sundays with them made her smile, and her heart felt full again.

Back at the cottage, Travis set down his car keys and removed his jacket.

After his proposal, they'd spent the remainder of the evening fielding congratulations from guests and hugs from the hotel staff.

Hallie—who felt like the little sister he'd never had—

had hugged him and said, "I knew you were too smart to blow it with someone as perfect for you as Riley."

It was a sentiment nearly everyone at Moonlight Ridge seemed to share.

Riley sank onto the sofa, "It's official. We're *really* getting married."

"Looks that way." Travis loosened his black bow tie, but left it hanging around his neck. He stepped behind the bar and pulled out two highball glasses. "Rum and Coke?"

"Please." Riley unstrapped her shoes.

Travis made their drinks, then handed her one before sinking onto the sofa, leaving an empty cushion between them.

"Regrets?" He sipped his rum and Coke, wishing he'd gone a little heavier on the rum.

Holy shit. He and Riley were about to get married.

"None." There was no hesitation in her voice. "You?"

Did he have regrets?

The public declaration of love wasn't his usual style. Yet, the moment they'd shared on that dance floor felt right and maybe a little too real. Like he was beginning to buy into the story they were selling.

This relationship wasn't real, and he needed to keep reminding himself of that.

"No regrets." He took a healthy swig of his drink as he watched her flex her feet, which were obviously in pain from the cute shoes she'd worn all night.

Travis set down his drink and reached for her foot, which she offered reluctantly. He gently massaged her arch.

Riley moaned softly, her eyes drifting shut.

He sucked in a deep breath and willed his body not

to react to the sensual sound. He massaged the ball of her foot with his thumb, then gestured for her to switch.

"You all right?" he asked. "About your parents, I mean?"

"That's the reaction I expected." She shrugged.

"Expecting it and experiencing it are two different things," he said. "Don't beat yourself up for being affected. They're your parents. The fact that it hurts just means you're human."

"I thought they'd at least *pretend* to be pleased in public. Of course, I didn't expect you to propose, let alone so publicly." She smiled sheepishly.

"You deserve your big, romantic gesture." He grinned. "Hope I didn't embarrass you too much."

"It was perfect and so sweet. I'll never forget tonight." A soft smile curved her sensuous lips.

The same lips he'd kissed earlier that evening. The lips he'd caught himself staring at since they'd returned to the cottage where they were playing a high-stakes game of "house."

He removed her foot from his lap and stood abruptly, running a hand over his head. "Been a long day for both of us. I'm exhausted. You must be, too."

He glanced at his watch. It was nearly two in the morning.

"I am." She seemed disappointed. "In fact, I'm too tired to get up and go to bed."

He could relate. Right now, his bed seemed a million miles away.

"Let me help you." Travis pulled her to her feet.

Riley gazed up at him, her hand still in his. "You were a superstar tonight, Travis. The gala and your proposal were amazing. I couldn't have asked for anything more.

Thank you." Riley lifted onto her toes and kissed his whiskered face.

But as she pulled away, Travis cradled her cheek, his heart racing as his eyes met hers.

He leaned down and covered her mouth with his. This kiss wasn't for the sake of anyone else. It was because he longed for another taste of her lips.

Riley tipped her chin, her lips parting. He swept his tongue inside the warm cavern of her mouth. The rum and cola mingled with the sweetness of the crème brûlée that lingered on her tongue. Her soft, warm body molded to his as he kissed her in the same room where he'd last kissed her all those years ago.

Riley made a delicious little murmuring sound that sent a jolt of electricity down his spine and he no longer remembered all the reasons he shouldn't do this.

They were two perfectly sensible, completely willing adults who'd be married for a year.

Why not give in to their desires?

Travis sank onto the sofa behind him, pulling Riley onto his lap. She hiked up the dress, giving herself room to straddle him, then wrapped her arms around his neck.

Their kiss grew hotter, more intense. Travis glided his hand up her outer thigh as Riley ground her hips against him. The warm space between her thick, brown thighs glided along his painfully hard length, both of them murmuring in response to the delicious sensation.

Travis glided the zipper down her back and kissed Riley's bare shoulder. She helped him shrug the garment down her arms, revealing a sheer black bra. He traced the stiff, brown peak with the rough pad of his thumb through the sheer fabric.

When he pinched the hardened nub, Riley gasped,

then bit her lower lip. Her brown eyes reflected every bit of the lust that coursed through his veins.

"Upstairs?" she whispered roughly, her chest heaving.

"Upstairs." He trailed kisses along her shoulder.

Travis stood suddenly, his hands beneath her perfect, round bottom as he lifted her. When he released her, Riley slid down his body until her bare feet touched the floor.

"Give me ten minutes, then I'll see you in my room." Her teasing smile was part vixen, part girl next door.

"See you in ten." He adjusted himself as he watched her ascend the stairs, her curvy form on full display as she clutched the dress to keep it from falling off.

Travis groaned quietly. He put away their glasses and turned off the lights downstairs before hurrying up to his room. After a quick refresh, he rummaged through his luggage.

He hadn't planned tonight. But given the increasingly flirtatious nature of their relationship, it seemed wise to be prepared. He tore into the box of condoms and stuffed a few into his pants pocket. Then he made his way down the hall.

He hesitated as he stared at her partially open bedroom door. The scent of Riley's body wash filled the hallway between her bathroom and bedroom. He wanted this, and evidently, so did she. He only hoped it wouldn't ruin the deal and the friendship they'd been rebuilding.

Seventeen

Riley paced the chilly hardwood bedroom floor in her bare feet.

After several torturous weeks of living with the man and behaving in public as if they were head over heels in love, her entire body burned at the thought of his rough hands gliding over her bare skin.

Sleeping together could change the dynamics of their business deal and tentative friendship in unpredictable ways. Yet, she couldn't regret giving in to the growing attraction between them.

"Hey, beautiful." Travis rapped his knuckle on her slightly ajar bedroom door and she nearly jumped out of her skin.

"Hey." Riley opened the door and stepped aside.

"I like what you've done with the room." He glanced

around at some of the shelving, wall art and knickknacks she'd added to the space.

"Thanks." Her stay at the cottage was temporary, but she wanted it to feel like home.

"Rye, if you're having second thoughts about this…" Travis shoved his hands inside his pockets and gave her a small, reassuring smile. "I understand. This thing between us is complicated enough as—"

No, no, no. Travis was talking himself out of this. Enumerating the reasons it wasn't the best idea. But her heart and her body were determined not to let her brain—or his—ruin tonight.

Riley gripped his white tuxedo shirt and tugged his mouth down until it crashed into hers.

She wouldn't let Travis talk her out of this. She wanted this deliciously handsome, incredibly brilliant and devastatingly sexy man on her, around her, inside her. It'd been all she could think about during the moments she lay awake tossing and turning in her bed at night, knowing Travis was asleep just down the hall.

Riley had spent her entire life being the sensible, good girl who did mostly what was expected of her. She thought of everyone else before herself, and she didn't regret that. But not tonight. Tonight, all she was thinking of was how her lips had tingled when Travis had given her that quick kiss in the elevator. And about how her entire body had burned with heat as Travis's mouth had slid across hers during their kiss in front of that crowded ballroom.

Travis wrapped his arms around her waist, tugging her closer. His hardened length pressed against her belly through the black lace nightgown she'd slipped on over a lacy thong after her quick shower. His hand glided down her back and cupped her bottom.

Their kiss began tentative and slow but quickly turned feverish. Her body ached with the need for his touch. Her nipples beaded and the space between her thighs pulsed. Soft, involuntary murmurs escaped her mouth as he deepened their kiss.

Riley shivered. Her skin felt as if it was on fire as his fingers dug into her flesh, pulling her into him with a sense of urgency that mirrored her own. She'd imagined this so many times.

Now, as his tongue glided against hers and they shared a hungry kiss, she couldn't wait to have Travis's hands on her heated skin. For him to touch her in the way she'd fantasized.

She unbuttoned his shirt and he helped her remove the garment. Travis tore his mouth from hers just long enough to tug his undershirt over his head and drop it onto the floor. Then he gripped the hem of the black lace nightgown and lifted it over her head. He cursed beneath his breath. His gaze trailed down her body and lingered on the hardened tips of her breasts.

Riley folded her arms over her chest, suddenly self-conscious beneath his heated stare.

"Don't." He lifted her chin and leaned closer. His breath warmed her cheeks. "You look amazing, Rye. I can't wait to taste every inch of that gorgeous brown skin."

"*Every* inch?" she teased. Her belly fluttered and her knees trembled at the thought.

"Every. Fucking. Inch."

The lascivious grin that kissed his sensuous lips had her heart beating double time and made her breath hitch.

Her brain was too preoccupied with the image of his mouth on her heated skin to respond.

Travis gripped her waist and lifted her onto the bed. His tongue danced with hers as his hands glided over her bare skin. Then he trailed slow kisses down her neck and down her chest. When his warm mouth covered one of the straining peaks, Riley whimpered softly. Her stomach tightened and her toes curled as her back arched. Her body demanded more of his kiss and his caress.

He willingly obliged.

Travis licked and sucked the sensitive peak as his free hand glided down her belly and into the space between her thighs that ached for his touch. He tugged aside the damp fabric, gliding his fingers over the sensitive nub. She shivered, as much in anticipation of what was to come as from the delicious sensation.

Riley clutched the bedding beneath her, her heart racing. Her heels dug into the mattress and her hips lifted. A silent plea for more.

He glanced up at her with a wicked grin that made her stomach flutter and set her skin on fire. Travis slipped one finger, then another, deep inside her, curling them. His fingers moved slowly at first, then more quickly, bringing her closer to the edge.

Her breath came faster, and her limbs felt heavy as Travis torturously teased one nipple, then the other. Then he kissed his way down her belly and over the black lace. Before her pleasure-addled brain could register what was happening, Travis pulled his fingers from inside her, replacing them with his warm tongue.

Riley gasped, her legs falling open wider and her hands resting on his head. His closely cropped hair tickled her palms. She rocked her hips and rode his tongue, greedy for more of the intense pleasure building low in her belly. Her knees shook, and her involuntary whimpers grew louder as Travis intensified his efforts.

She'd tried to hold it together. Held back the desire to scream his name loud enough to rattle the old windows and be heard by the guests in the neighboring cottage. But when he added his fingers again, the competing sensations were more than she could take. When he sucked on the distended bundle of nerves, she shattered into pieces as she called his name.

Riley lay there, breathing heavily, her muscles tense, her sex contracting. Liquid warmth spread up her torso. Her skin tingled all over. Travis lay next to her on his side, his large hand splayed on her belly. He sank his teeth into his lower lip as he studied her.

His stubbled cheek scratched her ultrasensitive skin when he leaned down and kissed her bare shoulder.

"Watching you fall apart is the hottest thing I have ever seen." There was a hint of reverence in his husky voice.

"I'll bet you say that to all the pretty girls you've been fake-engaged to." Riley stroked his cheek, then pressed her lips to his. He tasted of her. Something about that made her want to purr like a territorial feline who'd just staked her claim.

"I've never been engaged—fake or otherwise." He kissed her again. "You?"

Riley didn't respond right away. They often talked about their lives and careers, but they hadn't discussed past relationships.

"I was engaged several years ago. I wouldn't cosign a horrible land deal, so Patrick called off our engagement." Riley absently stroked Travis's stubbled cheek.

"My father and grandfather were right. He'd only been in it for my family's money. That's what prompted my grandfather to add the 'man of means' marriage clause to his will."

Compassion filled Travis's dark eyes. "Sorry things didn't work out, Rye."

"I'm not. It hurt when Patrick ended it, but I'm grateful the marriage didn't happen. I'm better off without him in my life, and if things had worked out…" Riley paused, thinking better of what she was about to say.

"Then you wouldn't be here with me now," Travis said the words she'd been thinking. His lips curved in a sincere smile that warmed her chest. He dropped a soft kiss on her eager mouth. "Then I guess I should be glad things didn't work out between you and what's-his-face."

Riley stared up at Travis's dark eyes, trying to read them. Did tonight mean as much to him as it did to her? Would this change things between them for the better or worse?

Her brain was trying to ruin their perfect night, but she wouldn't let it. Instead, she pressed her mouth to his. Lost herself in his kiss. Luxuriated in the warmth of his brown skin beneath her palms as she glided her hands down his back and gripped his firm bottom.

Kissing this incredible woman was Travis's new obsession. He'd really tried his best to keep emotional distance between them and to keep his hands to himself whenever they were here alone in the cottage, away from prying eyes. After all, this was a business deal, not a relationship. That was what they'd agreed to. And yet… Here they were.

They'd steadily been building a friendship. But since

the night they'd gone to dinner with her parents there had also been something more building in the background. Something deeper and more personal.

Tonight had been inevitable. Because for the past few weeks, their growing desire had been impossible to ignore, no matter how hard they tried. But despite all the reasons he knew he should, Travis could no longer hide his desire for Riley.

Maybe this relationship wasn't real or lasting, but tonight he would push all of those fears aside and allow himself to enjoy being with her.

Travis tore his mouth from hers, their chests heaving. He stripped off her lacy thong, then rolled off the bed and quickly shed his remaining clothing. He retrieved the strip of foil packets from his pocket and sheathed himself before joining her beneath the comforter on the chilly fall night.

He captured her mouth in a greedy, devouring kiss, his hands roaming over her soft skin and voluptuous curves. Her fingers dug into his low back and then traveled lower as she pulled him closer.

Travis gripped the base of his length, stretched tight and aching with need for this woman. He slowly pressed inside her wet heat, and Riley arched her back on a quiet gasp. Her nails dug into his biceps as she cursed beneath her breath.

Travis inched inside her as her body adjusted to his. Both of them murmured in response to the deliciously sweet sensation of their first connection. She held on to him, softly whimpering his name as her hips moved with his. Pleasure simmered low in his belly and rolled up his spine. His breath came faster, and his pulse raced as he moved inside her. Learning her body, as she learned his.

He circled his hips, supplying the friction she needed against her slick, engorged clit. Until her body went stiff and she called his name. Her sex pulsed, intensifying the already overwhelming sensations. His hips moved faster until pleasure erupted low in his belly and rocketed up his spine.

Travis tumbled onto his back and lay beside her, both of them spent. He gathered Riley in his arms, his heart still racing. "That was incredible, Rye."

"It was, wasn't it?" Riley's eyes gleamed in the low light cast from her bedside lamp.

Her cheek was pressed to his chest. Her hand was splayed on his stomach, inches from his cock, already stirring again from holding her in his arms like this, her velvety soft skin gliding over his.

"I thought it was just me because I've been fantasizing about this since I was sixteen," she admitted. "And then the fact that we're staying in *this* cottage—"

"I know," Travis said wistfully, not wanting her to say the words aloud.

Almost as if it was fate for us to cross paths again.

It was a thought that had danced around his head one day when she was sitting with him at his father's dining room table. Maybe their meeting had been serendipitous. But it wasn't fate. They still lived very different lives in opposite corners of the country. And there would be no happy ending for them. But they could enjoy their time together now.

He excused himself to clean up and discard the condom, taking longer than the task required as he thought about the awkward conversation they needed to have. About what this meant or didn't mean for them going forward.

Travis returned to the bedroom. "Riley, I think we should—"

She sat up suddenly, waving a hand to silence him. "Did you hear that?"

"Did I hear what?"

Suddenly, there was an urgent knock at the front door.

"Who would be here at this hour?" Riley whispered.

"Someone at the wrong cottage?"

There was another, more persistent knock.

"I'd better see who it is before they wake the guests next door." Travis slipped on his pants and undershirt. He kissed her forehead. "I'm sure everything is fine, but—"

"Be careful." Riley pulled the cover up over her chest and settled against the headboard.

Travis could see Hallie through the window at the top of the door.

Why would Hallie come to his cottage at this time of night? None of the reasons he could think of were good.

He called to Riley to let her know everything was fine. Then he opened the front door, his heart racing a little. "Hal, what's up?"

"Sorry to bother you, Travis, but it seems urgent." Hallie took a quick glance at his rumpled clothing and bare feet. "I would've called, but you left your phone in the office."

"What's the big emergency?" He stepped aside to let her in.

"You've gotten a bunch of calls and text messages from a Rosemary. That's your agent, right? She's been trying to reach you all night. When I saw the words *urgent* and *prospective investor*, I thought I'd better bring you the phone." Hallie handed it to him.

His lock screen showed the missed phone calls and

text messages from his agent and an email from Autumn confirming the date for his and Riley's wedding there at Moonlight Ridge.

He thanked Hallie and said good-night before listening to the first of Rosemary's three voice mails.

A potential investor for the New York restaurant was flying in from Germany. He wanted to meet Travis at a few potential sites in New York in approximately twelve hours. Rosemary had already booked him on an early flight out of Charlotte, which gave him about an hour to throw together a suitcase and hit the road for the airport if he was going to make the flight.

The investor's timing couldn't be worse.

Travis traveled frequently, so he kept his overnight bag stocked, and he'd become an expert at packing in minutes. He went to his room, packed his bag and changed into jeans and a long-sleeve shirt. Then trekked to the other end of the hall.

Riley exited the bathroom in her short, hooded robe. She'd swept her spiral curls up into a topknot and she was wearing her cozy slippers. His mouth curved in an involuntary smile.

"Not the sexiest thing, I know." She secured the belt. "But you left and it's cold tonight."

"I happen to think you look incredibly sexy in those cat ears and bunny slippers." Travis slipped his hands around her waist and kissed her. "And I'm sorry I had to leave."

"And yet, that kiss felt more like goodbye than an invitation to round two." Riley raised one of her perfectly arched brows as she gazed up at him. "Let me guess... business calls."

"I'm headed for the airport. I'm meeting a potential investor in New York."

"How long will you be gone?"

"A day, maybe two." Travis traced a finger along her exposed collarbone. "Will you be here when I get back?"

"No, I'm spending a few days with a sorority sister in San Francisco ahead of my conference there. From there, I fly to Holland for an international conference where I'm a presenter. You obviously don't consult the shared calendar my assistant set up for us."

He didn't. But now wasn't the time to admit that.

"Autumn was able to book our wedding in three weeks. You cool with that?"

"Yes, and I'm taking your advice and letting her handle everything. Just ask her to keep it simple and elegant."

"I will." He kissed Riley again, reluctant to leave his new fiancée behind. "Then I guess I'll see you a few days before the wedding."

"Guess so." Her sad smile made Travis's chest ache. He grabbed his bag and headed downstairs, already missing the gorgeous woman who would soon be his wife.

Eighteen

Riley sat at the bathroom vanity in Moonlight Ridge's bridal suite. Her wedding was an hour away. She'd wanted to keep the ceremony city-hall simple, but Travis suggested that a small wedding party would make the wedding seem more legit.

Mack and Grey were Travis's two best men, but her two closest sorority sisters were both pregnant. One was on bed rest. The other was due to deliver any day now. Neither could attend. Autumn and Molly had been gracious enough to stand in as her maid and matron of honor. Which meant Autumn, her wedding planner, was doing double duty.

"Everything okay?" Autumn stood behind her in the mirror.

The other woman tried to sound upbeat, but Riley

could hear the pity in her voice. Autumn felt sorry for her—alone on her wedding day.

"Everything is perfect." Riley felt the need to reassure Autumn she was fine without her family there.

But it wasn't true.

There was a hollow ache in her chest. This wasn't the fairy-tale wedding she'd always imagined, filled with family and friends. Instead, she was preparing for a hurried ceremony she'd barely had a hand in planning, and none of her family would be there.

Riley and her parents didn't see eye to eye on much, but it broke her heart that they weren't there with her.

Maybe this wedding had begun to feel too real because she had developed a deep, genuine attachment to Travis. Still, neither of them had defined what the relationship had morphed into. And the geographical distance between them the past few weeks had heightened the awkward tension.

"I wish every bride of mine was this calm on her wedding day," Autumn said.

Molly came into the bathroom, her curls glossy and perfect. Her smile was tentative. "Riley, you have a visitor."

"Who is it?"

"Me."

Riley's eyes flooded with tears when she heard the familiar voice.

"Nana?" She stood, squeezing the older woman's hand. "What are you doing here?"

Her grandmother cupped her cheek and smiled. "You didn't actually think I'd miss my only granddaughter's wedding, did you?"

Tears spilled down Riley's cheeks faster than she could blink them away. "Dad said none of you would be here."

"Last I checked, *I'm* still the matriarch of this family," Mariah George said firmly.

Riley hugged her grandmother. "Thanks, Nana. You being here means the world to me."

"I know, sweetheart," her grandmother said. "Can we talk alone for a moment?"

Autumn ushered Molly out of the room and closed the door behind them.

Riley guided her grandmother onto the stool in front of the vanity. "What is it, Nana?"

"This is about the money, isn't it?" Her grandmother squeezed her hand.

"You think Travis is marrying me because I'm an heiress?" Riley worded her question carefully.

"I think you're getting married to receive your inheritance, and you chose Mr. Holloway to antagonize your father." Nana chuckled.

Riley didn't want to lie to her grandmother. But could she trust that she wouldn't report back to her father? Maybe this was her dad's last-ditch effort to stop the wedding.

"Why would you think that, Nana?"

"Because it's *exactly* what I'd do in your position. But I would've done it two years ago."

Her grandmother cackled when Riley's eyes widened with surprise. "Don't worry, we'll keep this between us. I hate that your grandfather put you in this position. I had no idea about this awful provision to your trust. I wouldn't have stood for it."

"I know." Riley patted her grandmother's hand, freckled with age spots.

"You're a sensible girl, so I'm sure you've thought of protecting your financial interests."

"We have a carefully constructed prenuptial agreement that protects both of our assets."

"Good girl." Nana George nodded proudly. "That proposal of his was quite romantic. A man like that can be trouble in an arrangement like this."

"It's not just *an arrangement*, Nana." Riley clasped her hands.

"What do you mean?" her grandmother asked.

"I'm in love with him." The admission surprised Riley. "I honestly hadn't realized that until just now."

"Does Travis feel the same?"

Riley's heart sank to her stomach. "I know there's something more between us."

"But neither of you are quite sure what that is." Her grandmother nodded knowingly. "Well, that *is* a dilemma."

Nana squeezed her hand. "Is Travis a good man?"

"Absolutely."

"Do you trust him?"

"I do."

"Then I must trust that he'll take care of my granddaughter's heart." Nana George pulled her phone from her purse. She pecked on the keyboard. "Now, let's see this wedding gown."

"Autumn and Molly were just about to help me get dressed." Riley dabbed beneath her eyes, hoping she hadn't ruined her makeup.

"Perfect." Her grandmother moved to open the door. "Because I'm not the only one eager to see you."

When Nana George opened the bathroom door, her mother, Gina, stood in the doorway. Her eyes were filled with tears.

"Hello, sweetheart." Her mother waved tentatively.

"Mom." Riley barely squeaked out the word before tears streamed down her face again. She stepped into her mother's embrace.

"Enough of that," Nana George said. "We need to fix that makeup. No granddaughter of mine is going to walk down the aisle with her makeup a hot, unholy mess."

Within minutes, Autumn brought the makeup artist back. Then her mother and Autumn helped Riley into her wedding dress. Once she was ready, the four other women wore huge smiles. Her grandmother's and mother's eyes were filled with tears.

"You look absolutely exquisite, sweetheart," her mother said. "Come see for yourself."

Riley stepped into the handmade Italian Kahmune nude pumps that flawlessly matched her dark brown skin, then stood in front of the full-length mirror. The skirt of the romantic lace ball gown swished around her. She slipped her hands in the pockets and admired the dress with its long illusion sleeves and deep, plunging illusion neckline. The detachable beaded belt cinched her waist. She turned around, looking over her shoulder at the full illusion back and covered buttons, before turning to face the mirror again.

"Not bad." Riley rearranged a few strands of her tousled beach waves.

"Sweetheart, you're stunning. And I'm not the only one who thinks so." Her mother handed her the phone. It was a video call with her father.

"You are so beautiful, Princess."

"Dad?" Riley walked to the other side of the room. "I thought you didn't approve of my marriage to Travis."

"I still say it's a mistake, but you're my only daughter. So if this is the man you choose to marry, I'd regret not walking my baby girl down the aisle."

"I won't allow you to make Travis or his family uncomfortable," Riley insisted.

"I promise to be on my best behavior." He winked. "Now c'mon. In this family, we aren't late for our own weddings."

Her father ended the call abruptly, but Molly opened the door and he was standing on the other side. He stepped inside the room and took her hands in his.

"Look at you." He drew in a shaky breath, the corners of his eyes damp. "You're the most beautiful bride I've ever seen." He kissed her cheek. "I hope that Holloway boy realizes what a gem he's getting."

"Dad, you promised."

"Okay, okay. You ready?"

"Almost." Autumn approached with an ivory comb set with pearls.

Riley recognized the comb as her grandmother's. It'd been a gift from her mother on her wedding day.

She thanked her grandmother as Autumn swept her hair back on one side and inserted the elegant comb. Then she slipped her arm through her father's and made her way down to the ballroom where she'd finally marry Travis Holloway—in real life, not just in her dreams.

Nineteen

Travis slipped on his gray Tom Ford tuxedo jacket and straightened his burgundy tie as he looked in the mirror on the wall of the conference room where he and his brothers waited.

He and Riley had negotiated this marriage and the guest list. They'd talked about the wedding, though they'd allowed Autumn to do most of the planning of it. Still, it felt surreal that in less than an hour, Riley George would become his wife.

Travis straightened the collar of his white shirt, then picked up the boutonniere—a pink mini orchid with a burgundy center—and inhaled the sweet, calming scent.

"Let me handle that." Mack took the boutonniere from his hands, which he now realized were trembling slightly. Mack pinned the flower to Travis's charcoal-gray trimmed lapel. "You all right, T?" Mack lowered his voice and frowned slightly. "Not too late to change your mind."

"I'm fine." Travis fiddled with his shirtsleeves.

Truthfully? He did feel uneasy. The past few weeks had flown past in a blur, and things between him and Riley were in an odd place.

The night he'd asked her to marry him at the gala had been perfect. Had they not been interrupted, he would've gladly spent the rest of the night making love to her. But despite countless phone and video calls, they'd spent very little time in the same room over the past few weeks. And when they'd spoken or spent time together, things felt...*awkward*.

Sex had changed the easy vibe between them.

Maybe the universe was warning him not to fall for Riley again. Because, he was, in fact, falling for her.

That would explain why his stomach was in knots and his head felt light. He was more nervous about this wedding than he'd been doing live demonstrations to packed convention halls or in front of a live audience of millions.

"You don't look fine." Grey's dark eyes twinkled. "You look a little woozy. Should I get you a drink from the bar?"

"I'm good." Real or no, Travis wasn't showing up at his own wedding lit.

Besides, he didn't need a drink. Everything was fine. He and Riley were friends with benefits who would soon become fake spouses.

Nope, not confusing at all.

"It's just nerves. He'll be all right," his father said. "Travis has got a gorgeous woman who is a total sweetheart waiting to marry him. Hell, he should be skipping down that aisle."

"Did Riley send you to ensure Travis didn't pull a runaway groom?" Grey asked.

"No, she did not." Jameson narrowed his gaze at Grey, giving him a silent reminder to behave, like when they were kids.

"I realize how lucky I am, Pops." Travis shoved his hands in his pockets.

"Good." Jameson patted his shoulder and smiled. But for a fleeting moment he looked sad. "I love you, son." The older man squeezed his shoulder, then turned to regard Mack and Grey, too. "The three of you mean *everything* to me. Don't ever forget that."

"We know, Pops." Travis hugged Jameson. Mack and Grey did the same.

"Well, c'mon. Let's do this. Can't keep my future daughter-in-law waiting."

"Yes, sir." Travis took a deep breath and followed his brothers to the conservatory, where they were really getting married—despite what Riley had been told.

Travis stood at the front of the event space with Mack and Grey beside him. When "Arioso," by Johann Sebastian Bach, began to play and Riley entered the conservatory on the arm of Ted George, his heart leaped in his chest.

He'd called Riley's grandmother—Mariah George—and told her how disappointed her granddaughter would be if her family wasn't at her wedding.

They could hate him all they wanted. He really didn't care. But he couldn't bear to see Riley hurting because of her family's notable absence from the ceremony.

The sadness in Riley's voice had been evident when

she'd mused about the possibility of this being her only wedding and her family not being there.

Riley presented a strong front, but her family's plan to snub their wedding cut her deeply. So he'd made the call to the George family matriarch, realizing it was a long shot. Despite his feelings about Riley's family, he was glad to see them there. The broad smile on his bride's face as she descended the aisle on her father's arm made Travis's heart swell.

Riley was stunning in her lace wedding dress with its plunging illusion neckline. Her hair fell to one shoulder in soft waves. The other side was swept back with a decorative hair comb.

His heart danced with joy at the wonder and surprise on Riley's face as she surveyed the space.

They were in the conservatory where they'd first laid eyes on each other as children. He'd been playing a game with his brothers and she and her mother were sitting on a bench beneath a sunny window reading.

There was something about her he'd instantly found mesmerizing. But he'd been a preadolescent boy who still thought girls were awful, annoying creatures who ruined everything. So he'd exchanged a polite smile and a nod with her—as he did with the children of all the guests—and continued playing Battleship with his brothers.

Years later, Riley told him she'd first fallen for him that day in the conservatory. He'd asked Autumn to plan a lovely, ethereal wedding there in the place where they'd first met. But they'd told Riley the wedding would be in one of the small ballrooms.

Travis wished he could've been there to see Riley's face the moment she realized they were getting married in this lush, green space. He followed her big brown eyes as they took in the conservatory. Sumptuous swaths of fabric hung overhead. Lush pink camellias, regal purple hyacinths and fragrant white orchids filled the place.

Autumn had outdone herself. And by the look on Riley's face, she felt the same.

Riley and her father now stood in front of him. Ted hugged his daughter, then kissed her cheek. He exchanged a stilted handshake and tense eye contact with Travis before stepping aside.

"You look gorgeous, Rye," Travis whispered as he extended his elbow to her.

Riley thanked him and slipped her arm through his as they stood in front of the officiant.

The ceremony was short and sweet. When it was time to exchange vows, his heart threatened to beat out of his chest. The corners of Riley's eyes were damp, and her voice trembled slightly when she spoke.

This wasn't the simple business transaction they'd agreed to. Nothing about their ceremony felt like an act. He had genuine feelings for Riley. Maybe not love, but something akin to it.

When they'd exchanged rings and the judge pronounced them husband and wife, Travis captured her mouth in a kiss. His lips glided over hers, and he wished they were standing alone in this beautiful space. That he could kiss her for as long as he pleased.

The officiant cleared his throat and chuckled.

Riley smiled, a slight look of embarrassment on her lovely face as she reached up to wipe the lipstick from his mouth with her thumb. Travis kissed her palm.

Her smile deepened and his heart felt...*full*. In a way it hadn't before.

Mack was right. He was definitely in trouble.

* * *

It was the end of the evening, and Travis watched as Riley chatted with her family. He was surprised the Georges had stayed to help them celebrate their wedding along with a room filled with family, friends, business associates and several of Moonlight Ridge's employees. Despite not practicing and winging a song choice, Riley even got her father-daughter dance.

Travis was happy for his new bride.

He and Ted had even declared a temporary truce. It'd nearly choked the man to say the words, but he'd shaken Travis's hand and congratulated them on their nuptials.

"Made nice with the in-laws, I see." Mack handed Travis a beer as they watched Riley saying goodbye to her family in the rotunda of the hotel, just outside the ballroom doors.

"Temporarily." Travis was under no illusion that he and Riley's dad would suddenly become friends. "But as long as Rye is happy on her wedding day, that's all that matters."

"You seem pretty damn happy yourself." Mack chuckled. "Who's that your wifey is talking to? I don't remember seeing her at the wedding."

Travis turned back to where his wife was standing. Her family was gone, and she stood in the center of the rotunda speaking with a woman who looked…familiar. He chugged some of his beer, before handing the bottle back to his brother.

"Excuse me, Mack. I need to take care of something."

"That woman looks a lot like the pictures of—"

"I've got this," Travis said, his voice tense. "See if you can get the DJ to play something that'll get the remaining guests on the dance floor."

"You've got it," Mack said. "Just don't do anything... you know...stupid." Mack put his large hand on Travis's shoulder. "And if you need me, I'm here."

Travis made his way across the rotunda.

"Here's my husband now." Riley's eyes lit up as he approached. "Travis Holloway, meet Lenora Nelson— your biggest fan."

Is that what she had convinced herself she was? His biggest fan?

Travis slipped a protective arm around Riley's waist as he regarded the woman cautiously. He surveyed her dark eyes and generous mouth, so similar to his own. His heart thumped in his chest and his temple throbbed.

Riley looked concerned when he didn't respond. She seemed to notice the tension in his muscles as he and the woman studied each other. Riley pressed one palm to his chest; the other rested on his back. A silent show of support, for which he was grateful.

"Travis." The woman's raspy voice was filled with emotion. "I can hardly believe it's you. It's been such a long time."

Travis stiffened his spine, and his fists clenched. He tried his best to convey zero emotion.

"It's been twenty-six years, *Ma*." He tried to strain the hurt and anger from his voice. She'd abandoned him without sending so much as a birthday card in all this time. She didn't deserve to know how deeply her abandonment had cut him. That it affected him still. "And you decide to show up today?"

Her eyes filled with tears. "I realize how hurt and angry you must be."

Travis looked through the woman. The ghost of a painful past. "I *was* hurt and angry. But now I'm over it."

Riley tightened her grip on him as she studied the other woman's face.

"Travis, sweetheart, I didn't leave because—"

"I'm not interested in your excuses anymore, Ma. You're two decades too late. You weren't there for me then, and I don't want you here now," he growled, lowering his voice. "This is a private family wedding. If you're still here in five minutes, you'll be escorted off the property."

Travis held on to his wife, as if she was his lifeline. He was embarrassed Riley had to witness his messy family issues. But he took comfort in her presence.

"I understand if you can't forgive me, Travis." Tears streamed down her cheeks. "But we need to talk."

"Please don't approach me or my wife again." He ignored her plea and turned to walk away, his arm still around Riley's waist.

His wife hesitated, pulling him aside. She slipped her hand into his.

"Baby, I'm sorry. I didn't know," Riley said.

"How could you?" He sighed. "Let's just go back and enjoy the rest of our night."

"Travis, you have every right to be upset. But you don't want to leave your mother out here making a scene in the lobby." Riley glanced around, likely looking for any members of the filming crew who might be lurking about. They'd gotten footage of the wedding and from earlier at the reception. But they would be back shortly to get footage of them saying good-night to their guests. "Nor do you want her to feel her only option to be heard is to go to the tabloids. They'd gladly run with a salacious story about a beloved celebrity chef *allegedly* mistreating his long-lost mother."

His heart rate slowed and the tension in his shoulders eased. Riley was beautiful and brilliant. A much-needed voice of reason.

He'd seen too many celebrities with asshole relatives determined to milk their fifteen minutes of fame for all it was worth. People who'd been shitty and absent their entire lives suddenly appearing on morning television shows and in tabloids, making it seem like they were the ones who'd been abandoned and mistreated.

Just months ago, Autumn's father—a sleazy Hollywood producer and general trash human being—had pulled a similar stunt on national TV. It had led to several wedding cancellations and jeopardized that side of the business. The last thing Travis wanted was to cause more negative publicity for Moonlight Ridge.

"What do you propose?" Travis swept her hair behind her ear.

"Let me talk to her. Maybe I can diffuse the situation," Riley offered.

Travis glanced at the woman he'd once loved more than anything. But her lack of response to his countless attempts to contact her over the years had made it clear he'd never really mattered to her.

It had been one more thing weighing on him as he'd lain in his hospital bed recovering from the accident. Feeling as if everything he'd ever wanted in his life was lost to him. Wondering if this had all happened to him because he wasn't worthy of love or happiness.

"I'm not leaving you alone with her."

"I appreciate your concern, but Nicky and Ricardo are right there behind the front desk and the valets are right outside. I'll be fine." She squeezed his hand.

Travis glanced at his mother again. "Don't go any-where with her and don't believe a word she says."

He'd learned that the hard way as a kid. So many times his mother had promised tomorrow would be different. He'd believed her and been disappointed every time.

He'd never forget the last lie of Lenora's that he'd be-lieved.

I'm just going to the store, baby. I'll be right back.

Travis had waited for his mother for two days before the social worker had arrived. He'd spent that two days trying to convince himself there was a reasonable expla-nation for her absence. And that she really did love him, even if she didn't show it in quite the same way other mothers did.

"Promise me." He needed Riley to understand how persuasive Lenora could be.

"I promise," Riley said. "Our marriage may not be tra-ditional, but we're a team, Travis. The night of the gala, you told me that you've got me. That I can rely on you to have my back. Well, I feel the same, so let me handle this for you. *Please.*"

Her dark brown eyes were so sincere.

Travis checked his watch. "We give our parting speeches in half an hour. If you're not back in fifteen minutes, I'm coming to check on you."

He kissed his wife's cheek, then headed back inside the ballroom without sparing a glance at the woman who'd decided her life was better off without him in it.

Twenty

Travis climbed out of the back of the turquoise-and-white four-door 1959 Ford Galaxie 500 hardtop convertible that once belonged to the original owner of Moonlight Ridge, Tip O'Sullivan. Then he helped his new bride out of the car.

Riley looked beautiful but exhausted after their full day. The reconciliation with her family. The wedding. The reception. Then meeting her new mother-in-law. She'd put on a big smile and returned to the wedding reception in time to thank partygoers and wish them a good night. But something about her seemed heavier. Sadder than before when she'd been floating on a cloud and he had, too.

It had brought him immense joy to surprise Riley with a fairy-tale setting for their wedding and to ensure that her family would be there. And when he'd stood in front of that officiant and declared that he loved and was committed to her, it hadn't felt like he was pretending at all. Little by little, almost without him noticing, it'd become the truth.

Riley was the only woman he thought of now. He cared for her. Worried about her. Would defend her at all costs. Just as she'd once made a huge sacrifice to protect him and his family. Even when it meant breaking her heart and his.

Their driver, Manny, a longtime employee of the hotel, snapped video and pics of Travis carrying Riley across the threshold—at Jameson's request. Then they bid Manny a good night.

While Riley made a mad dash to the restroom, Travis transported their bags to their rooms. He removed his jacket, loosened his tie and sat on the edge of the bed.

Travis had worked hard to push every memory of his mother from his brain. Because remembering even the good times reminded him of all the pain. For his own mental and emotional health, he'd chosen to forget Lenora Nelson ever existed. So, of course, she'd turned up again to churn up all of that pain on what should've been one of the happiest days of his life.

It was strange to see his mother again. To hear her say his name. He'd engaged an emotional force field the moment he'd recognized her. And he'd kept himself from telling her what he thought of her in excruciating detail.

Because Jameson Holloway had raised him better than that.

I know you're angry, Travis. But she's still your mother, son.

He could hear his father's words in his head. Travis was glad Giada had taken Jameson home by then. The idea of those two worlds colliding always made him uneasy. As a teenager, Travis hadn't told Jameson about his attempts to reach out to his mother. A part of him felt as if reaching out to Lenora was a betrayal of the man who'd given him everything: a home, a family, a future and unconditional love.

Jameson Holloway had always treated him and his brothers as if they were his own flesh and blood.

Travis fought back the memories of his mother. His anger was the lid that kept all of the pain those memories conjured at bay. His mother's rejection had shredded his heart to pieces. But eventually, his raw, bleeding heart had formed a callus. Maintaining his hardened feelings toward Lenora had become his coping mechanism. His way of protecting his heart.

Yet, part of him wanted to demand answers to the questions that'd plagued him for years: Why had she abandoned him? Had he been that awful a child? Did she just not want a kid?

Travis had gone to bed each night with those questions burning a hole in his chest for much of his life. But the only thing more devastating than not knowing the truth was being told more lies. So he'd pass on whatever his mother had come there to say.

Still, her reappearance had reaggravated his old hurts. Torn loose the stitches that tenuously held together those jagged wounds.

"Sorry to bother you." Riley stood in the doorway. The light from the hallway glowed around her like a halo. "But it took two women to get me into this dress. I'm going to need a little help getting out of it. Would you mind?"

"No." Travis stood, sliding the tie from his neck. He tossed it on the chair with his suit jacket. "Come here."

Riley walked over to him, then maneuvered the large skirt as she turned around, giving him her back. She swept her hair over one shoulder as she glanced back at him. "Think you can handle it alone?"

He whistled, assessing what looked like one hundred covered buttons trailing down the sheer back of the dress. "They've got you strapped in here good."

"I know. If I'd sneezed, there's a good chance someone would've lost an eye tonight." She laughed, patting her stomach.

"Good thing you didn't." He chuckled, slowly working through the task obviously meant for someone with slimmer fingers. Meanwhile, an awkward silence descended over them again, like a heavy, wet shroud.

"There." He'd unfastened the last of the buttons on the back of her dress. "All done."

"Thanks." She held the top of the dress up with one hand and lifted the bottom with the other.

"You were beautiful in that dress, Rye. Excellent choice."

"Thank you." She stared at him a moment in the mostly dark room. "We need to talk about my conversation with your mom—"

"I don't want to talk about her." He cut her off abruptly.

The soft, gauzy moment between them was shattered by her mention of his mother. But it was Lenora he was angry with, not Riley.

"But she said—"

"I've heard all of the lies, all of the excuses. I don't want to play those tired games anymore. So whatever sad story she's told you to garner your sympathy, Riley,

I don't want to hear it. All right?" He shoved his hands into his pockets.

"Okay." Riley agreed reluctantly. "And thank you for today. Having the ceremony in the conservatory was such a sweet surprise, and it meant a lot to have my family there. My grandmother told me about your stern lecture." She laughed. "You've certainly earned my Nana's respect. I can't thank you enough."

Travis's family had embraced Riley, and she seemed to appreciate that. But the sadness in her eyes whenever the topic of her family came up… It was something he could relate to. So he'd been prepared to do anything short of dragging Ted George's ass out of his house to ensure he was there to walk his daughter down that aisle.

Riley lifted onto her toes and kissed his cheek.

He studied her face. She was beautiful. Thoughtful and sweet. His family adored her, even if hers would just as soon see him dropped off the end of a pier.

And for at least the next year, they'd committed to being together.

When Riley had proposed this wild scheme, being married for a year to a woman he'd loathed sounded like being condemned to his personal hell. But after getting reacquainted and learning he'd been wrong about her, his feelings were completely different.

"What happened with your mom tonight is a lot to process. You'd probably like some time alone." Her tone indicated she hoped otherwise.

Maybe he did need time alone to process the pain and trauma Lenora Nelson's sudden appearance had revisited upon him. But that wasn't what he wanted.

Not tonight.

Tonight, he wanted to be with the woman who consumed his every thought.

"Don't go, Rye. Stay, *please*."

Riley stared at him wordlessly from beneath her thick lashes. She released the lacy garments, allowing them to pool around her bare feet.

She stood before him, naked from the waist up, wearing only a blinged-out scrap of fabric masquerading as panties. His cock twitched and his belly tensed.

Tonight, he fully intended to have Riley George-Holloway back in his bed, and there would be no interruptions.

Twenty-One

Riley's pulse raced as Travis's dark eyes locked with hers then slowly glided down her body. He held his hand out to her, and she took it, stepping out of the wedding dress. He helped her gather the frothy, lace confection and its underpinnings, draping them over the chair with his tuxedo jacket.

Travis closed the distance between them and pressed his mouth to hers. His hands moved to her bare back as he cradled her body to his. Her lips parted as she looped her arms around his neck. Travis accepted the invitation, his warm tongue gliding along hers. He held on to her tightly. Kissed her with a ravenous hunger that caused her sex to pulse.

He swallowed her quiet murmurs as he cradled her jaw. His kiss sent shivers down her spine that set her entire body on fire. The damp space between her thighs throbbed and her nipples beaded, scraping against his hard chest.

Travis's hooded gaze radiated abject desire. "Riley, you look absolutely amazing."

He captured her mouth in a kiss that made her feel that every kiss she'd received before this one had been amateur hour. He kissed her until she was breathless.

Travis's strong hands trailed down the sensitive skin of her bare back. He squeezed her bottom, pulling her flush against his hardened length pinned against her belly. He cursed beneath his breath in response.

When he lifted her, she instinctively wrapped her legs around him. Travis carried her to his bed and laid her down. He kissed her, his tongue searching hers as he teased one hardened nipple with his thumb.

Travis glided down her body, covering the nipple he'd been teasing with his warm tongue and grazing it with his teeth. The sensation went straight to her sex, already pulsing with her growing desire for him. When he trailed soft, slow kisses down her body, Riley's belly fluttered in anticipation.

Travis tugged off the sheer thong and kissed the space between her thighs, eliciting an involuntary gasp. She shuddered as electricity shot up her spine.

Travis's tongue glided over her swollen, aching flesh, bringing her to the edge. He stopped just short of her coming undone, giving her a small reprieve. Just as her heartbeat started to calm down, he went in for more. Travis repeated the cycle again and again. Each time, he drove her higher, the feeling more intense than before. Until she was trembling and cursing as she clutched the duvet. Begging him to let her come.

"All you had to do was ask." His eyes glinted with

a wicked grin. His lips glistened with evidence of her pleasure.

Riley didn't just ask. She pleaded, begged and perhaps even threatened. She wasn't quite sure. Because at some point, she'd been on the edge of losing consciousness.

Travis slid two fingers inside her, his movements precise, as he continued to use his mouth to bring her the most incredible pleasure. Finally, her body tensed, and her inner walls pulsed as she called his name until her throat was hoarse.

He seemed to recognize when she'd reached her maximum threshold for pleasure. Travis eased off, finally removing his fingers and placing one last kiss on her slick, sensitive flesh. Then he trailed kisses up her belly before lying beside her. Travis wrapped her in his arms, flipping the duvet over them.

She laid her cheek on his chest, ruining his white shirt with her makeup. She'd buy him another. Because right now, there was no place she'd rather be than in her husband's arms.

They lay together in silence, her pulse still racing, and her heart beating wildly. As amazing as Travis had made her feel, her body vibrated with need. She was quickly becoming shamelessly addicted to this man, her husband.

Riley kissed Travis slowly, unbuttoning his shirt as their kiss grew more heated. They worked together to strip Travis down to his underwear. When he stood and dropped those, Riley nibbled on her lower lip as she regarded the ridiculously sexy man she'd spent the past several weeks fantasizing about. She could recall with great detail every kiss and every touch from their memorable night together.

But this moment was about more than her growing

desire for Travis. When they'd stood in front of their friends and family and repeated their vows, she'd meant them. She wouldn't be satisfied with a fake marriage. She wanted Travis in her bed and in her life. *Period.*

Now she only needed to make him see how good they could be together, too.

Travis gazed at his beautiful wife. Everything about Riley George-Holloway was soft and comforting. Her smiling face and open expression instantly warmed his chest.

It had taken cajoling, coaxing, a guilt trip and flat-out bribery to get him to agree to this marriage. But it had taken none of that to get him to stand in that conservatory today awaiting the beautiful woman who'd first captured his heart nearly two decades ago. Because he truly cared for Riley and he looked forward to their time together.

Travis sheathed himself beneath the appreciative gaze of his wife. They crawled beneath the covers and he kissed Riley, his tongue searching for hers. He loved the feel of her soft skin and the sensuous sounds she made as he trailed kisses along her shoulder. The way her back arched when he teased the hardened tips of her full breasts with his tongue.

Travis kissed his way down her stomach, to the valley between her thick thighs. He used his lips and tongue to bring her to the edge again. Until she was begging to feel him inside her.

He obliged, reveling in the delicious sensation of her body, soft and warm, opening to him as he inched inside her. Loving the sweet, torturous sensation of Riley dragging her perfectly manicured nails down his back. Marking him as hers.

She held on to him, her wide eyes filled with heat as they moved together. He wanted to hold on to this moment and to the passion building between them. But when Riley's body tensed, his name on her lips as her inner walls spasmed and she tumbled over the edge, he could barely hold on.

He quickly found his release, waves of pleasure overwhelming his senses as his heart hammered inside his chest.

Travis tumbled to the mattress beside his wife, gathering her to his chest. The room was silent, but the moment didn't feel awkward, as it had before. Instead, there was a feeling of quiet contentment.

He'd been living alone for so long, he'd forgotten what it was like to have someone to come home to. Someone to cook a special meal for: his language of love.

Travis kissed the top of Riley's head. "Sex won't make this weird, will it, Rye?"

"I'm fake-married to my childhood sweetheart." Riley raised her head and laughed. "I'm pretty sure it can't get any weirder than this."

"Guess you've got a point." He chuckled softly.

But the truth was nothing about today felt fake. Maybe that was the weirdest thing of all.

Twenty-Two

Jameson Holloway rocked on the back-porch swing. He studied the trees turning various shades of red, orange and gold. Autumn was always gorgeous there in the Blue Ridge Mountains. He never took for granted how fortunate he was to be here. He loved his work, and he was lucky to have become the father of three fine men.

Moonlight Ridge and his boys had kept him too busy to think of love or marriage. There had been dalliances over the years. But nothing serious enough to make him consider sharing his life with someone.

Of course, he wished he hadn't almost died. But he was grateful for everything that'd happened since then.

All three of his boys had come home. One by one, they'd found love with women who couldn't be more perfect for his sons if he'd handpicked them.

Mack and Molly were happily married, and Mack's

new brewery was opening that night. Jameson expected Grey to propose to Autumn any day now. Travis and Riley were returning from their honeymoon later that afternoon—just in time for the grand opening of the brewery.

When the boys had gotten in that accident, he'd never been more frightened in his life.

Afterward, Travis had been so angry. At his brothers. At Riley. At the world.

Jameson had tried to be a good father to his sons. But he'd been so focused on Travis's recovery that he'd left Mack and Grey to struggle with the fallout on their own. The physical distance between the boys had increased their emotional distance. Travis was angry and bitter about losing his football career. Mack and Grey were scared of losing control and disappointing the people they loved. All three of them had focused on their careers and avoided close personal connections.

A chasm formed between his sons. For him, that had been the biggest tragedy of the accident. One he hadn't known how to fix.

So, if it had taken what had happened to him to reunite Mack, Grey and Travis and remind them how much they loved each other, he couldn't regret that.

"I brought you some hot chocolate." Giada appeared in the doorway, her eyes twinkling.

Giada was the other reason he couldn't regret his illness. It had brought this beautiful woman, whom he'd always adored, back into his life. And as she'd taken care of him these past months, they'd fallen in love. Something he had yet to admit to his sons.

"Sounds perfect, sweetheart." Her decadent, thick Italian hot chocolate was a rare treat. How could he possibly say no? Jameson patted the space beside him on the swing. "Join me?"

"I'm still working on the appetizers for the opening at the brewery tonight," she said in her lovely Italian accent. "But I did bring you some company. An old friend, Lenora Nelson."

Jameson's eyes widened and his gut tightened. He climbed to his feet. "She's here. *Now?*"

"Yes, she is waiting in the front room. I thought I would bring her out here to join you." Giada frowned, stepping onto the back porch and lowering her voice. "Is there a problem, *caro*? Should I send her away?"

"No. You did the right thing, sweetheart." Jameson kissed her cheek. "Please send her out. Thank you."

Giada looked at him strangely. *"Va tutto bene, amore mio?"*

"Yes, darling." He stroked her cheek. "Everything is just fine. I promise."

Giada pressed a kiss to his lips, something he would never tire of. Then she smoothed his shirt before turning to walk away.

Lenora Nelson.

That was a name he hadn't heard in years. The last few times he'd thought of her, he'd hoped and prayed she was out there and still alive. For Travis's sake. Because he realized that at some point in his life, Travis would want to reconcile with his mother.

His son had tried to keep it a secret, but Jameson knew he'd tried to reach out to his mother several times over the years without success. Lenora just hadn't been ready to meet with her son. Hadn't wanted him to see her the way she'd been the last time she'd shown up there to beg him to take Travis in and raise him.

The screen door opened and Giada ushered Lenora out onto the porch. She gave him a questioning look, but he nodded to indicate she needn't worry.

"Hello, Jameson," Lenora said once Giada was gone. "It's good to see you again."

He wished he could say the same. But his gut told him otherwise.

"You're looking well, Lenora." Jameson sat down. He gestured for her to sit in a padded wicker chair opposite the swing. "What can I do for you?"

"We need to talk about our son," she said.

Jameson glanced toward the kitchen window. Could Giada hear their conversation?

"What would you like to talk about?"

"I spoke with him." She sat down heavily.

"When?" Jameson scooted to the edge of his seat.

Travis and Riley had been away in the Maldives on their honeymoon. The first week had gone so well they'd decided to stay a second week.

"The night of their wedding," Lenora said.

"You crashed their wedding?"

"He's *my son*, Jameson," Lenora said defensively. "Why should I be considered an intruder at my own son's wedding?"

Because you weren't invited.

"I realize it must've been upsetting to be an outsider at your own son's wedding, Lenni," Jameson said. "But *you* created these circumstances. What did you expect? You cut the boy out of your life and now…*what*? You thought he'd be okay with you popping in at his wedding?"

"You're right, I know." Lenni studied her hands, folded in her lap. "Travis should be upset. If he'd told me how angry he was, I would've gladly taken it. But the way he looked at me. It was so…cold. Like I meant nothing to him." Her eyes welled with tears.

Jameson handed Lenni one of the napkins Giada had set on the table, and she dabbed her face with it.

"What *exactly* did you say to him?" Jameson's gut tightened in a knot.

He'd been bone-tired the day of the wedding. Giada had made him leave before the reception ended. But the entire family had brunch together the following morning before Travis and Riley left for the airport.

He was hurt that his son hadn't mentioned his encounter with his mother.

"I tried to apologize and tell him I'm ready to rebuild our relationship." She sobbed, dabbing her cheeks. "But he wants nothing to do with me."

His heart ached for her, but his son was his primary concern. "You didn't tell Travis—"

"No." She shook her head. "But he needs to know."

"It was you who insisted that I not tell him," he reminded her.

"I know." Her dark eyes, a carbon copy of Travis's, were filled with agony and regret. "It was a mistake. You were right. I should've told him."

"Telling him now… Do you have any idea what that will do to him? He's finally gotten over all of the anger and blame related to the accident. Travis and Riley have just begun their new life. Don't disrupt his happiness, Lenni."

"Whatever time I have left on this earth, I plan to use it to reestablish a relationship with my son. But we can't build that relationship on a lie, Jameson. I *have* to tell him."

"Think of how this will impact him. It'll turn his entire world upside down. Please, just give it a little more thought, and I promise I'll try to get Travis to at least talk to you. All right?"

Lenora frowned, then she sighed.

"I only want what's best for Travis. So I promise to consider what you've said."

"That's all I ask." A little of the tension rolled off Jameson's shoulders, but the knot in his gut was still firmly in place.

Whatever happened, he only hoped that his son wouldn't withdraw to that same dark place he'd gone to after the accident. Not when he'd finally found love and rediscovered the importance of family.

Lenora took her leave, and a few minutes later, Giada returned. She slid onto the swing beside him and placed a comforting hand on his leg.

"What is wrong, Jameson?" she asked in her melodious accent.

Jameson didn't respond. Instead, he held her hand. He wanted to tell Giada everything. But if he was going to talk to anyone about this, Travis deserved to hear it first. So he couldn't tell Giada. Not yet. But he could tell her the other truth he'd been holding inside for weeks.

He turned toward her and stroked her cheek. "I wish I could tell you everything, sweetheart. But right now—"

"I understand," she said. Her warm assurance that everything would be okay made his heart feel lighter. "This woman… She is Travis's mother?"

Jameson sighed heavily and nodded.

Giada leaned into him, still holding his hand. "Then we do not need to talk about it."

"I'm so grateful to have you back in my life." Jameson studied the woman's face through the haze of emotion that filled his eyes. "And this time, I won't let you go without a fight. I love you, Giada."

Jameson cleared his throat, then cackled. "I'm too damn old to get down on one knee. And don't feel you have to answer me right now, but will you—"

"Yes!" Giada interrupted his rambling. "Before we get any older...*yes*, Jameson Holloway. I would most happily marry you. I love you, too."

Jameson kissed Giada. He held her in his arms as they watched the sun set over the mountains in the distance. His heart was filled with a deep sense of joy and happiness. The woman who'd become his best friend and constant companion these past few months had agreed to be his partner for the rest of their lives.

But beneath the joy and happiness was the unshakable feeling that a storm was brewing on the horizon.

Twenty-Three

Travis checked the three trays of mini crumb-topped berry pies he had baking in the oven at the women and children's shelter. He and Riley had returned from their honeymoon in the Maldives one week earlier.

They'd spent two weeks swimming, lying in the sun, exploring local foods and culture, spending quality time together and making love. If it hadn't been for work and community obligations, they might've stayed another week.

"Need help in here?" Riley poked her head into the kitchen.

"Actually, I do need something. Come here a sec?"

"Sure, babe. What is—"

He pulled her into his arms, taking her by surprise when he kissed her.

"Nice." Riley wiped her tinted gloss from his lips. "Save that energy for when we get back home."

"You better believe it." He winked.

"Chef Travis, I… Oh, I'm sorry. I didn't mean to interrupt." Joan, the director of the center, hurried into the kitchen. "But the volunteer manning the smoker thinks the meat might be ready and he's afraid of overcooking it."

"I'll be right there." Travis still held his wife in his arms. He kissed her forehead.

When Joan left the kitchen, Travis gave Riley a pat on the bottom, and she laughed. Then he followed Joan through the kitchen doors.

Travis checked on the meat and gave the volunteer in charge of the smoker additional instructions. He turned back toward the kitchen but halted when a familiar voice called his name.

He turned toward his mother, who was wearing a volunteer T-shirt. "What are you doing here, Ma?"

Travis glanced around, thankful the film crew was elsewhere, capturing B-roll for the show. Still, there were local news crews on-site.

"Volunteering." She stepped closer.

"Don't pretend you didn't know I'd be here."

"I did. But I'm also here because this place was here for me during a really tough time in my life. I like to give back whenever I can, however I can."

"You spent time here?" He hadn't wanted to engage her, but he couldn't help himself. He knew very little about her life after she'd disappeared from his.

"Yes. My life was a roller-coaster ride for a while. One I couldn't take you on. Because you deserved a happy, stable life. The kind of life Jameson Holloway was able to give you."

"You had no idea where I'd end up. I could've been placed with abusive foster parents or ended up on the streets." His shoulders tensed and his temple throbbed. All of the pain and anger came rushing back, making it difficult to breathe. "But you didn't care. All you cared about was yourself."

"That isn't true, sweetheart." His mother's dark eyes filled with tears. "I did what I did *because* I loved you. I wasn't in the right emotional state to care for you. I tried, baby. I really did. But I was in a downward spiral. I had to do right by you, so I placed you in foster care until I could get on my feet again."

"Then why didn't you come back for me?"

"It's complicated," she said. "But I never stopped thinking of you."

"If that were true, you wouldn't have gone ghost on me." Travis rubbed at the gnawing pain in his chest. "But the real question is, why are you here now? What is it that you want?"

"I have so many regrets in my life. None more painful than how I hurt you. I want to make things right with you, Travis." She wiped at the tears spilling down her cheeks.

He'd fallen for her tearful promises that things would be different time and again as a kid. He wouldn't fall for the waterfalls and bullshit again.

"I have to get back to the kitchen." Travis turned abruptly to leave.

"Wait! There's something you need to know." Her voice was loud enough to garner attention from a few nearby volunteers.

Travis gritted his teeth, his wife's words echoing in

his head. He didn't want his mother to make a scene. He turned around. "What is it that you just have to tell me after all this time?"

Uneasiness crept down Travis's spine in response to his mother's expression. It was the same tortured look he'd seen whenever she'd had to tell him a painful truth; the kind that would change everything. His father was terminally ill. Their home was being seized by the bank.

What horrible news would she deliver this time?

"Are you in some kind of trouble? Do you need money?"

"Jameson Holloway is your father," she said.

"Of course he is. You agreed to the adoption. It was the only time you responded to—"

"No, Travis." She pressed a hand to her forehead. "Jameson is your *biological* father."

There was one person in his life who'd *never* disappointed him. Whom he could always trust. And that was Jameson Holloway. So what she was saying *had* to be a lie.

"You stay out of my life for more than twenty years and this is the kind of nonsense you come at me with? Why? What could you possibly hope to gain?"

"It's true, sweetheart." Lenora sighed. "I met Jameson at a concert in Atlanta one summer. We hit it off and shared one incredible weekend together. Then I returned to my life in Raleigh and he returned to his here. We never expected to see each other again."

She rubbed her arms. "A few months later, I realized I was pregnant. By then, I'd met your dad—Doug," she clarified. "We'd gone out a few times. When I learned I was pregnant, I tried to break it off with him. But when I explained why, Doug just smiled. He said he'd fallen in love with me the moment he'd laid eyes on me, and that he'd always wanted children but couldn't have them. So rather than breaking up with me, he asked me to marry him." A soft smile lit her dark eyes. "Best decision I ever made."

"To marry Dad?"

"And to have you," she said.

He couldn't accept what his mother was telling him. Not because he didn't want to be Jameson Holloway's biological son. But because it meant everything he believed about his life was a lie.

Still, the uneasy feeling in his gut told him it was true.

"Does Jameson know?" Travis's voice was faint.

"He didn't at the time, and if Doug had lived, he'd never have known," she admitted. "We were such a happy little family, you, me and Doug. I couldn't risk losing that."

"When did Jameson learn about me?" Travis's stomach was tied in knots.

Lenora sank onto a nearby bench. "At the time, we lived in Raleigh. Your father surprised us with a weekend trip to Asheville, and we stayed at Moonlight Ridge. That's when I saw Jameson again. I was in shock. I'd never expected to see him again. You weren't quite three. Jameson took one look at you and he just…knew," she said. "I was terrified he'd try to take you away from us, so I denied you were his son and lied about your age so he wouldn't put it together."

"Did Dad know Jameson was my father?"

"Yes, I never kept anything from Doug. He agreed we shouldn't take a chance on Jameson fighting for custody. But he was glad we knew where to find your biological father, in case you learned the truth as an adult and wanted to know him."

Travis dropped onto the bench, his legs collapsing under the weight of her confession. He felt hot and cold at the same time. His head spun and his mouth felt dry.

"He's known since I was three?"

"He *suspected* as much then. I didn't confirm the truth until after your father was gone. We were about to lose the house, and I was unable to cope with losing the love of my life." His mother wiped away the tears streaming down her face again. "I had nowhere else to turn, so I came to Asheville and told him the truth, and that his son needed his help. He found us a place here and paid the first six months of rent. He wanted to get to know you. I thought we should ease into the relationship, but never tell you Doug wasn't your real father."

"And he agreed to that?" Travis's jaw clenched.

"Only because I threatened to disappear with you if he didn't. Soon afterward, things began to spiral out of control for me. In a moment of clarity, I explained my situation to a social worker who lived in our building. She talked to Jameson. Helped him get qualified as a foster parent. We made arrangements for him to care for you, if ever I couldn't."

So Jameson had known he was Travis's father long before he'd arrived at Moonlight Ridge. He'd never indicated as much. Nor had he treated him any differently than Mack or Grey.

Travis was stunned. Inside his head he was howling like a wounded animal. Yet, he had to maintain a calm facade in this very public place with the television crew and members of the media roaming around.

"I need to talk to my dad."

"He already knows I planned to tell you. So does she." Lenora nodded toward Riley, who approached.

"There you are, babe. Joan sent me to look for you because—" Riley stopped abruptly when she saw the expression on his face. That's when she recognized his mother.

She looked like she'd seen a ghost.

Riley lowered her gaze, her chin dipping to her chest as she smoothed back her hair.

"Mrs. Nelson." Riley's smile faltered. "Lovely to see you again."

"You knew?" Travis stood, facing her.

The sound of his heart thumping in his chest filled his ears. When his mother dropped this bombshell in his lap, his first reaction was that he needed to talk to Riley. To seek the comfort and advice of the woman he adored. Yet, for the past three weeks she'd already known. And she'd never said a word.

"I had no idea that your mother was volunteering here today," she said quickly.

Travis lowered his voice so the curious group over by the grills wouldn't overhear them. "You knew that Jameson is my real father?"

Riley shifted her gaze to his mother, then back to him, leaning in closer so only he could hear her. "I knew your mother *claimed* Jameson was your real father, and I tried to tell you as much at the cottage that night. You refused to hear me out, and you insisted I shouldn't believe her. So I thought I should at least talk to your dad first."

"And did you talk to my dad?"

"No, I… I planned to but… I…" Riley stammered. "I was worried about how it might impact your relationship with Jameson."

"You mean you were worried I'd back out of this deal. That I wouldn't be willing to sacrifice a year of my life to help my father restore Moonlight Ridge if I knew he'd been lying to me since I was seven."

"You think I kept this from you for selfish reasons?" Riley looked hurt. "Travis, I'd never do anything to intentionally hurt you."

She reached out to him, but he stepped backward, sinking onto the bench again.

He closed his eyes, shutting out their competing voices. Both women were apologizing and insisting he should let them explain. But the reality was they'd both kept the truth from him and so had Jameson.

He'd spent much of his life struggling with an inability to trust people. The one person he'd *never* doubted had been Jameson Holloway. And he'd slowly begun to trust Riley again, too. But his trust had been misplaced. Neither of them had been honest with him.

Travis stood abruptly, angry with himself for forgetting the lesson he'd learned at seven. The only person he could consistently rely on was himself.

He lowered his voice to a harsh whisper.

"I have an obligation to fulfill here." He looked at his wife pointedly, making it clear their marriage was one of those obligations. "We'll talk about this later."

He offered his open palm to Riley, who reluctantly placed her hand in his.

They'd been behaving like newlyweds who were madly in love all morning. If any tension between them was detected, breakup rumors would be online before he'd served dessert.

So instead, he'd smile and behave as if nothing had

changed—despite the fact that his entire world had just imploded, and it felt as if there was no one in his life he could truly trust.

Twenty-Four

"Travis, say something, *please*." Riley spoke over the roar of the Hellcat's engine. They were nearly back to the cottage, and he'd barely said two words to her.

"What do you want me to say, Riley? That I'm disappointed in my mother, Jameson and you for not telling me the truth?" He shrugged. "That seems pretty damn obvious."

Riley wished Travis would just get angry. Tell her what he was feeling. Then they could fight, make up and move forward *together*. Instead, Travis was punishing her with a silent disdain that indicated he'd written her off.

Her heart ached at the thought.

Lenora and Travis had put her in an awful position, leaving her with no good choice. Riley had handled the convoluted situation in the way she thought best. She hadn't done anything wrong. Yet, given Travis's past, she understood why he'd taken her silence as betrayal.

"I'm sorry. If there was even a sliver of a chance that what your mother said was true, you deserved to know."

"Then why didn't you tell me, Riley?" he demanded. "And don't say it's because I didn't want to know. I didn't want to hear your marriage proposal, either, but that didn't stop you."

Direct hit. Like when she'd watched Travis and his brothers playing Battleship when they were kids. She needed to be honest with her husband and herself.

"That night at the cottage... What happened between us was so perfect. After everything we've been through, we were finally together and happy. I was terrified of screwing that up. And I've put off talking to your dad because I adore Jameson. I didn't want to hurt or embarrass him."

Travis turned into the drive leading to Moonlight Ridge. "Well, there's no avoiding that, huh, Princess?"

No, it didn't seem there was.

Travis walked into the house where he'd grown up. A place that had represented love and family. For a time, he and his brothers had forgotten that. But since their father's illness, each of them had rediscovered the importance of family.

Yet, a single conversation with his mother threatened to shatter it again. Because right now, it felt as if he'd walked into the house of a stranger.

"Hey there, son. How'd the banquet at the women's center go?" Jameson grinned.

"The event went fine," Travis said curtly, ignoring

Trouble and Nonsense, who'd gathered near his feet, waiting to be greeted. "But we need to talk."

There was a look of realization in his father's eyes. Suddenly, Jameson Holloway looked every bit of his sixty-five years.

Jameson settled onto his favorite chair in the den as Travis sat opposite him. "I'm guessing you've spoken with your mother again."

"So it's true?" Travis felt like he'd been run through with a spear.

"Yes. I'm your biological father. I have the DNA test that proves it."

"How could you keep this from me? And why would you pretend to take me in out of the kindness of your heart when I'm *actually* your son?"

"You're all my sons," Jameson said. "And yes, my blood runs through your veins, Travis. But I honestly couldn't love any of you more than I do."

"I appreciate that, Dad." The word hit differently now that he knew Jameson was his real father. "But I still don't understand why you'd allow me to believe I was another man's son."

"You *are* his son, Travis. Douglas loved you, as surely as I do. Your mother didn't want to ruin your memory of him, so she made me promise not to tell you. It was the only way she'd agree to let me see you. So I promised her, and I've kept my word. No matter how badly I wanted to tell you."

The last time Travis had heard this kind of pain in his father's voice was when he'd been fading in and out of consciousness after the accident. He didn't want to hurt Jameson, but this conversation couldn't be avoided. And Travis had every right to be upset.

It was honorable of Jameson to keep his word to his mother, but Travis had the right to know the truth.

"I won't pretend to understand why the three of you kept this from me or to be okay with it." Travis's head throbbed. He could only imagine the anxiety this conversation was causing his father, who was still recovering. Travis studied his father, who was clearly distressed. "How are you feeling, Pops? Physically, I mean?"

"I'm fine, son." Jameson sighed. "But I'm sorry. We should've told you long ago. I realize you're angry with your mother and me—"

"And Riley," Travis said.

"Why Riley?"

"My mother told her the night of the reception. Riley did try to tell me that night, but I didn't want to hear anything my mother had to say. So Riley backed off and never brought it up again. Not once in three weeks." Travis grew agitated thinking of all of the opportunities Riley had to tell him the truth.

"Son, I understand why you're miffed with me, your mother and Douglas. But if Riley tried to tell you and *you* insisted you didn't want to hear it… Son, that's on you," Jameson said matter-of-factly. "Don't use this as an excuse to blow up what you have with Riley. You two were meant to be together, Travis. Look how happy you've been the past few months. A love like that doesn't come around too often. When it does, you'd best grab hold of it. Don't let a pigheaded misunderstanding destroy what you two have."

Travis set back on the sofa and sighed. His father was right; he'd put Riley in an impossible situation. She'd done as he asked. Yet, he'd accused her of keeping the truth from him. No wonder she'd looked hurt and bewildered on their ride home.

Guilt roiled in Travis's chest. He'd been unfair to his wife. But as he stared at his father now, he realized he was being unfair to him, too. He was angry Jameson had kept him in the dark about his paternity. But he was just as wrong for concealing the true nature of his marriage to Riley from his father.

Travis swallowed hard and met Jameson's gaze. Then he told his father the truth about Riley's dilemma and the financial proposal that resulted in their marriage. Something she'd given him permission to share with Jameson from the outset.

After his initial shock, his father listened patiently. Then he asked about a few details of the arrangement as it pertained to Moonlight Ridge.

"Thank you for leveling with me, son. But I have to be honest, I'm not comfortable accepting help on those terms. Though I suspect you already knew that." Jameson sighed. "But I'll tell you what I do know. Riley is an amazing woman. When I met her as a kid, I hoped she wouldn't let her family's money and elitist attitude change her, and she hasn't. She's doing so much good in the world and in our community. And it's obvious she truly loves you. I believe you love her, too."

"I do," Travis admitted quietly. It was a realization that had slowly been building over the past two months.

"Then tying your relationship to a financial arrangement—"

"Is a recipe for disaster?" Travis rubbed his stubbled jaw. "I know. I've been thinking about that since we got married and I realized…"

"That this wasn't an act anymore?" His father chuckled quietly. "Coulda told you that way before then, son."

"I haven't touched her money. Nor have I made plans to move forward with the restaurant." Travis ran a hand over his head. "It just didn't feel right."

"Good." His father raised a triumphant fist. "I know you find it hard to trust people, Travis. I'm sorry if keeping your paternity a secret has added to that lack of trust. But please don't let an inauspicious start or a miscommunication ruin the love you two have built."

His trust issues were the reason he'd been quick to attribute a selfish motive to Riley. Travis had struggled with his lack of trust his entire life. He'd entered every friendship, relationship and business deal with an eye on the exit. Expecting the other party to disappoint him the way people in his life often had.

"You and your brothers mean the world to me, Travis. It brings me so much joy to see the three of you finding love and being a family again. Molly, Autumn and Riley are the daughters I never had. Seeing you build families of your own with such incredible women…" The corners of Jameson's eyes were wet. "*That* is the greatest accomplishment of my life."

There was so much love and pride in Jameson's misty eyes. His mother's revelation had been shocking. But in the end, both Jameson Holloway and Douglas Nelson were still his fathers. They were good men who'd loved and cared for him. And they'd done what they'd believed to be in his best interest. He was lucky to have had both men in his life.

"I should get home and talk to Rye." Travis stood. His father stood, too, and Travis hugged him tightly. "I love you, *Dad*."

Jameson patted his back. "I love you, too, *son*."

"I guess we should tell Mack and Grey."

"Only if you want to. Like I said, it doesn't change a thing. I'm still as much their father as I am yours."

"I know. But I don't want there to be any more secrets in this family."

"Good." Jameson scratched his gray beard, a slow smile spreading across his face. "And on that note, I need to tell you boys that I've asked Giada to marry me, and she said yes."

"I knew you two were getting close, but *wow*. I'm really happy for you, Pops." Travis smiled. "I'd say Giada will make a great addition to the family, but she's already become an important part of this family. And after all of the sacrifices you've made for the three of us, I'm glad you're finally getting your happy ending, too."

"Thank you, son." Jameson smiled, then rubbed his beard, in deep thought. "I know you're eager to get back to your wife, but I have an idea. Can you spare a few minutes?"

"Sure, Pops." Travis could see the wheels turning in his father's head. He returned to his spot on the sofa. "What's on your mind?"

Twenty-Five

Riley had spent the past two hours at the cottage making a few phone calls and replying to pressing emails. Beyond that, she couldn't concentrate enough to get any real work done.

She couldn't control what Travis thought or was feeling. So she focused on something she could control. Riley was cleaning and reorganizing her office—located in the guest room. If Travis's silent treatment on the way home was any indication, she may very well find herself sleeping there again.

But she couldn't control that, either.

What she would do is dig in her heels and stake her claim. Riley didn't want a loveless, fake marriage that made them both miserable. She wanted the love and friendship they'd been developing over the past few months—even if they'd both been too afraid to call it that. Fate had conspired to bring them together again after all this time. She wouldn't give up on this so easily.

Riley stopped what she was doing when she heard the distinct roar of the Hellcat pulling up to the cottage. She descended the stairs just as Travis entered the front door.

"Hey." He shoved his hands into his pockets.

She stood at the foot of the stairs, her arms folded. "Hey."

An awkward silence lingered between them, then they both tried to speak at once.

"Travis, I…"

"Riley…"

Travis gestured toward her. "You go first."

Riley sucked in a sharp breath and stepped forward. She met his gaze. "I admit to having selfish reasons for not forcing the conversation. Our wedding night was like a fairy tale, and I didn't want to burst the bubble. I was terrified that if I did, we'd never get the magic of that night back. So I sat on the news, and for that, I'm sorry."

"Riley, I—"

"I'm *not* finished." She pointed.

He snapped his mouth shut and gestured for her to continue.

She had to get this off her chest before she lost her nerve.

"You are a fucking adult, Travis Holloway. You said… no, you *insisted* you didn't want to hear what your mother said. You were adamant that I shouldn't believe anything she told me. Now you're angry with me for doing *exactly* what you asked me to do. I'm your wife, Travis. Not your nursemaid. I'm not here to coddle you. And I may have a lot of talents but being a mind reader isn't one of them. You need to say what you mean and mean what you say."

Riley huffed, her words running together so quickly she was out of breath. When he didn't interrupt, she continued.

"The day we stood in front of everyone and said our vows… That never felt fake to me, Travis. Because what I feel for you is real. I'm in love with you." The words came out in a strangled whisper. "Not just because you were my first love. Because I love the man you've become. You're an ambitious entrepreneur. Yet, you were willing to make this huge sacrifice for your family. You've become so invested in the community since your return. You've unselfishly taken Hallie under your wing, and you treat her like a sister. You're kind and respectful to all of the hotel employees. And I love spending time with you and your family. I've never been happier, Travis. And it seems like us being together makes you happy, too."

"I definitely should've gone first." Travis rubbed the back of his neck.

"Why? What were you going to say?" She searched his unreadable expression.

"That I'm sorry for being an asshole. You're right. You did exactly as I asked." Travis stepped closer. "I've got some shit I'm still trying to work out, and it was wrong of me to take that out on you." Travis lifted her chin, then he kissed her, his calloused thumb grazing her cheekbone. "I love you, too, Rye."

Tears stung Riley's eyes, and a slow smile spread across her face.

"Forgive me?" He brushed his lips over the backs of her fingers.

"Of course." Riley stared up at her husband through the haze of unshed tears. "But if we're going to make this work, we have to be honest with each other about everything."

"I know." Travis took her by the hand and pulled her over to the sofa. "And if we want this to be a real marriage, I can't accept your money. That's why I haven't touched it or made plans for the restaurant. Also, I leveled with my dad about our marriage arrangement."

"Your dad." Riley pressed a hand to her chest. "I was so focused on what I needed to say that I forgot to ask how your talk with Jameson went. Are you two all right?"

"We're good," Travis said. "But he feels the same way. He won't take money from you as some kind of payment for our marriage."

She should be flattered her husband didn't want her money, but she loved Travis, and she loved Moonlight Ridge. The place felt like home, and Jameson felt like family.

Riley wanted to be a part of that.

"You need my investment to complete the renovations, and converting the old café into one of your signature restaurants is a longtime dream of yours." Riley squeezed her husband's hand. "I have the money. I adore Moonlight Ridge. And I believe in the Holloway men. I want to see this place thrive again while your dad is still around to see it, Travis."

"We all want that." A warm smile slid across her husband's handsome face. "That's why my dad proposed that you be given a proper stake in Moonlight Ridge."

"Your father is letting me be an investor in the property?" Riley was stunned, knowing Jameson had been adamant that only family members should invest in the estate.

"Pops is making you a *partner* in the estate—just like

every other member of this family who has invested in
Moonlight Ridge. And I'm offering you the same in the
restaurant." Travis's smile widened. His eyes shone with
emotion as he kissed the back of her hand. "I want you
as my partner, Riley. In life, in Moonlight Ridge and
in my restaurant here on the estate. If that's what you
want," he added.

"That's exactly what I want." She nodded enthusias-
tically, wiping away the tears of joy that wet her cheeks.

Riley was genuinely excited about partnering with
Travis in his new restaurant. She wanted to be a part of
this new venture—the intersection of two things that
meant so much to her: Travis and Moonlight Ridge. The
place where they'd met, gotten married and were currently living.

"In fact, I think we should celebrate." Riley slid onto
her husband's lap, straddling him.

"Is that right?" Travis's large hands settled on her
hips. His voice was gruff. He wet his lower lip with his
tongue. "What did you have in mind, Mrs. Holloway?"

Hearing him call her that made her heart dance, so
she didn't bother to remind him that her name was hy-
phenated. For tonight, she was perfectly content to be
Mrs. Travis Holloway.

Riley teased him with a soft, playful kiss. But Travis
tightened his grip on her bottom as his lips glided over
hers. His tongue searched her mouth.

Her tight nipples grazed his hard chest and she moved
against the growing ridge beneath his zipper as their
kiss became more intense. The space between her thighs
grew slick and ached for his touch. Her skin tingled and
warmth swept up her neck and face as their kiss became
more urgent.

Riley pulled her mouth from his. Her knees were shaky as she stood. "I'm taking a shower…in case anyone is interested."

She headed for the stairs, hoping her husband would be right behind her.

Travis watched his wife ascend the stairs looking like pure sex wrapped in a sweet, angelic bow. In no time flat, he was off the sofa and had joined her in the bathroom they now shared. They worked together to remove each other's clothing between frantic kisses.

He brushed his lips over the glowing brown skin of his wife's shoulder. Riley was a stunning woman with her delicious curves. The pebbled peaks of her soft, full breasts made his mouth water. She had a curvy ass that could stop traffic, tantalizingly thick thighs and hips made to hold on to. She had warm, expressive eyes and a mouth he simply couldn't get enough of.

Riley stepped into the running shower and crooked a finger in invitation. The sexiest smile lit her brown eyes.

Travis joined her, pressing his hands to the shower wall on either side of her. He gazed down at this amazing woman. He could still hardly believe she was his wife. That she'd be sharing his bed every night for the rest of their lives.

Riley made his days so much better with her brilliant mind, sweet disposition and teasing sense of humor. Her mere presence brought him a sense of contentment.

Travis captured Riley's mouth in a kiss that set his body ablaze with desire. His already stiff cock grew harder pressed against her soft belly, and he couldn't wait to be inside her again. He slipped his fingers between them, gliding them over her slick folds and teasing her sensitive flesh as he avoided her clit. Her breath came in short pants, and he swallowed her moans of pleasure during their feverish kiss.

Her murmurs escalated as he increased the pace and pressure of his touch, taking her higher and driving her insane with pleasure. Finally, he caressed the taut bundle of nerves with his thumb as his fingers glided in and out of her.

Riley's eyes shot open. Her mouth formed a little O. His spine tingled with the visceral memories of all the amazing things that sexy little mouth could do. Riley rode his hand, her breathy pants indicating she was close.

There was nothing sexier than his wife on the brink of orgasm. He got off on watching her. On knowing he was the one bringing her such mind-blowing pleasure.

"Omigod, omigod, omigod...*yes*." Riley's legs shook and she leaned into him as she came hard, her inner walls gripping his fingers as she called his name.

Every last ounce of his control snapped. He whispered in her ear, "Baby, I need you."

Travis flattened Riley's palms against the tile wall, lifted her foot onto the shower bench and entered her from behind. Both of them moaned with pleasure when he slid inside her and hit bottom.

The feeling so deliciously intense, it took every ounce of control he could muster to glide in and out of her wet heat with a slow, steady rhythm. His fingers glided over her clit, bringing her to the edge again.

Riley's body tensed and her inner walls pulsated around his heated flesh as she called his name.

He thrust harder and faster, until his muscles tensed, and he came hard, whispering his wife's name in her ear as he emptied himself inside her.

Travis's chest heaved, both of them panting as he dropped to the bench, pulling her onto his lap. He kissed her shoulder, his head still spinning. Travis had one clear thought running through his mind: he was thankful to have Riley in his life, and he'd never let her go.

Later, they lay in bed after making love again. They'd spent the evening opening up to each other in ways they hadn't before.

Riley explained why she wanted to get her hands on her inheritance. She hoped to help save two charities that didn't yet meet the criteria to receive funding from their family foundation. It affirmed what he already knew: Riley was a selfless, amazing woman and he was damn lucky to have her back in his life.

He revealed that there was an embezzler within the ranks of the Midnight Ridge employees, and they were closer to uncovering who it was. Riley was as outraged that someone had been stealing from Jameson as he and his brothers were.

"Tell me what you've done so far to catch this person." She went from her soft, dreamy, post-sex mood into business mode in two seconds flat.

He updated her on what they'd done thus far and shared their suspicions that it was someone connected to the kitchen or catering.

Riley scrolled through her phone, then she typed out a message. "I'm calling in a favor."

She told him about a guy named Edge who was a fixer her father sometimes used. His methods weren't always *traditional*, but according to Riley, his results were impeccable.

"You sure about this?" He twirled a lock of her hair, still damp from the shower, around his finger.

"It's what we do for family, right?" She stroked his stubbled cheek.

Travis's heart expanded. "Have I told you how much I love you, Rye?"

"Repeatedly." She grinned. "Especially while I was doing that thing you like with my—"

"Don't say it." He kissed her. "I'm getting hard again just thinking about it."

Seriously, the things this woman could do with her mouth.

Travis cleared his throat. "Okay. Do it."

"Are we talking about engaging Edge's services or—"

"Both." Travis sank his teeth into his bottom lip, his dick tenting the sheet.

Riley grinned. "*That*, sir, is the right answer."

Twenty-Six

Travis scrunched his six-foot-two frame behind the wheel of his Hellcat. He and his brothers were parked on a narrow street in a nondescript part of Spartanburg, South Carolina, a little more than an hour southeast of Asheville.

"We should've rented a fake laundry delivery truck," Grey piped from the back seat. "That's what they do on cop shows. Besides, it would've been more comfortable."

"One of us is cracking under the pressure of this mission," Mack said from the front passenger seat.

"We should've brought a coloring book and snacks to keep him occupied," Travis teased.

"I'm fine back here, thanks, *unfunny* guys," Grey muttered.

"You should be. You've got the whole damn back seat to yourself," Mack grumbled.

"Shh…" Travis held a finger up to his lips. "Shit's about to get real."

A tall man climbed out of his sedan and ran his hands through his thinning brown hair. Two other men approached and shook his hand. He led them to his trunk and opened it.

"I hope this works," Grey said.

"That bastard better pray the cops arrest him before I beat the shit out of him," Mack said.

"Ditto." Travis echoed his brother's sentiments.

It'd been killing them to watch this creep move about the hotel each day for the past week, knowing he'd been stealing from their father for years. But they'd agreed this was the best way. He'd be caught red-handed and have to pay for his crimes.

The two men looked inside the trunk, inspecting its contents. Finally, the taller man nodded his approval and the shorter man handed Ross Barnes—the catering manager at Moonlight Ridge—a thick wad of bills.

Ross grinned wolfishly and counted the bills before stuffing the wad inside his jacket. He shook the taller man's hand again. This time, the man wrenched Ross's hand behind his back and cuffed it while the shorter man held a gun on him. The undercover officers told Ross he was under arrest for theft and attempting to sell meat on the black market.

The camera crew suddenly emerged from their undercover van and captured Ross's arrest for the show.

Edge had unraveled the complicated money trail left by Ross and his girlfriend—a brilliant former accountant who'd done time for embezzlement. Ross had been purchasing silverware, linens and other items, then stealing them and selling them on the black market.

Mack, Grey and Travis stepped out of the car and ventured closer, eager for Ross to know who was responsible for his current dilemma.

"I'd like to punch him in his smug face." Mack stared Ross down.

"Do you think he knows he's fired?" Grey smirked at the man.

Ross dropped his head as a uniformed officer led him to a patrol car.

Travis and his brothers got back into the Hellcat. He texted his wife to let her know they'd caught their thief and were headed home. He couldn't help smiling at her response. He was head over heels in love with Riley and grateful to have her in his life. When he glanced up, his brothers stared at him with knowing grins.

"What?" Travis started the car and headed back to I-26W toward Asheville and Moonlight Ridge. Toward the place and the people that felt like home.

"Marriage looks good on you, Travis," Mack said.

"You too," Travis replied.

"We're three incredibly lucky guys." Grey's broad grin filled the rearview mirror.

Travis couldn't help but agree. They were all very lucky men indeed.

Travis had recounted the details of his stakeout with his brothers to Riley while she helped him make dinner. Now he handed her a slice of the butter pecan layer cake she'd been impatiently awaiting. He was considering adding it to the Traverser restaurant menu.

Riley eagerly scooped a forkful of the moist cake into her mouth and purred. "God, Travis. This is so good."

Travis felt the sensual sound deep in his gut. A flush

of heat crawled up his neck. He sank onto the sofa beside Riley and she fed him a bite of the cake.

"It's amazing, right?"

Travis shrugged. He was trying out a new recipe. It was good, but not perfect. He'd keep working at it.

"Your dad is going to love this," Riley muttered through a mouthful of cake. "In fact, it's going to be a hit with the entire family."

"You think so?"

"I know so." Riley kissed his lips. Suddenly, her mood was less bubbly. She set her plate on the table. "Speaking of family, there's something I need to say about your mom."

"Okay." Travis put his plate down, too. They'd avoided the topic of his mother for the past two weeks, since Lenora had dropped the bomb about his true paternity. He turned to her. "Let's hear it."

Riley turned toward him. She folded her legs on the couch and placed her hands in his.

"I can't imagine how much it hurt to have gone through what you did as a kid. But when we were at the shelter, I realized that several of the women there have stories similar to Lenora's."

He grunted but didn't interrupt.

"Your mother was battling anxiety, depression and grief as she struggled with losing the love of her life. She self-medicated to numb the pain. Just like many of the women there that we've committed to helping." Riley squeezed his hand. "Baby, I'll support whatever decision you make. But I can't help thinking—"

"I should extend my mother the same grace," he finished her thought.

It was a fair point. One Jameson had already urged

him to consider. How could he forge a future with Riley without dealing with his past trauma around trust and relationships?

This second chance they'd been given meant everything to him. He had no intention of blowing it.

"I'll think about it."

"That's all I ask." Riley kissed him.

"Mmm… That butter pecan cake does taste good on you." He pressed another kiss to her lips, and she giggled in response.

Travis pulled Riley onto his lap and nuzzled her neck. He resumed their kiss, fueling his insatiable hunger for this stunning, brilliant woman he was so lucky to have in his life.

Piece by piece, their clothing drifted to the floor. He made love to his wife. Something he would never tire of.

"I love you, Rye," he whispered, holding her close. "I don't ever want to lose you again."

"You won't," she assured him as they snuggled together on the sofa beneath a cashmere throw. "Because I love you, too, Travis. And I'm never, ever letting you go."

Travis had never been happier.

He finally had the love, friendship and family that had been missing from his life. So he would hold on to them, and to her, for as long as they lived.

Epilogue

Travis stood in the kitchen of Traverser at Moonlight Ridge—set to open in time for the holidays. He checked on the beef Bourguignon, a perennial favorite at his restaurants. Travis fanned the steam and inhaled the aroma from the Cognac, red wine, carrots, pearl onions and garlic. It smelled divine.

He nodded his approval to Lathan, his executive chef. Then he instructed his sous chef, Rosa, to remove the red fluted ramekins filled with cranberry orange crème brûlée from the fridge. Once the creamy custard confection reached room temperature, he'd pull out his butane torch and caramelize the crème brûlée himself, creating the perfect sugary crust.

As Travis glanced around the state-of-the-art kitchen,

buzzing with his recently hired staff, he was filled with a sense of pride.

Little more than a year ago, Riley had mused about the café being converted to one of his restaurants by that time next year. Sure enough, the expansion of the building to its larger footprint had been completed by then. And in a few more days, Traverser at Moonlight Ridge would open to the public.

Tonight, he and Riley were hosting the annual Moonlight Ridge staff holiday party at Traverser. The event was doubling as a dry run for their grand opening later that week.

Travis slipped on his navy blue dinner jacket and returned to the dining room. The old café was completely renovated and decked out in festive holiday decor. The place buzzed with joyful conversation and laughter, and Travis couldn't help smiling.

Serving his first meal in the new space to the people who'd become his family filled his heart with immeasurable joy.

"Everything good, Dad?" Travis squeezed his father's shoulder.

Jameson was seated at one end of the long table, holding the hand of his wife, Giada, seated beside him. "Couldn't be better, son."

"The bacon-wrapped scallops and creamy cauliflower and bacon soup were *delizioso*," his stepmother said in her lilting Italian accent as she kissed her fingertips in a chef's kiss.

"Thank you, Giada." It was high praise from such a brilliant cook. His stepmother's abilities in the kitchen, coupled with his father's utter contentment, had contributed to the slight tire around the old man's waist and his ever-present grin.

Travis was grateful to have both of them in his life.

He turned to his brothers. "I hope you saved room for my beef Bourguignon and dessert."

"Absolutely." Molly's green-gray eyes sparkled as she rubbed her burgeoning belly. She leaned into Mack, whose arm was wrapped around her. In just a few months they'd welcome the first of the next generation of Holloways. A baby boy they'd already named Landis. "I am eating for two, after all."

Travis squeezed his brother's shoulder as he walked past, and Mack grinned proudly in response. It was good to see Mack so happy.

He glanced over at Grey, who gazed dreamily at his wife as they chatted. After a brief engagement, he and Autumn had gotten married over the summer in the rose garden at Moonlight Ridge.

Since the completion of the renovations, Moonlight Ridge had become a premier destination for weddings and for Sunday brunch—keeping both of his sisters-in-law and their expanded staff busy.

Travis surveyed the space. Three long tables were filled with his family, key members of the Moonlight Ridge staff and their loved ones. Without their dedicated team, Moonlight Ridge would never have made its incredible rebound during the past year.

Travis nodded at Hallie, seated between her grandmother and younger sister. He was incredibly proud of how she'd blossomed into her role as Moonlight Ridge's executive chef. And with the limited-run reality series about the hotel's renovation airing soon, he had no doubt Hallie's star would continue to rise.

Travis slid into his seat at the head of the table and squeezed his wife's hand. Riley George-Holloway was beautiful, as always. Her glamorous, red sequin dress popped against her dark brown skin, and her hair fell in silky waves over one bare shoulder. His love for Riley grew exponentially every single day of their lives together. He gave his wife a quick kiss on the cheek as the restaurant staff brought out the main course and began serving it.

"You've outdone yourself, son." Travis's mother, seated to his left, beamed. "And I'm so very proud of you."

"Thanks, Mom." Travis kissed her cheek. He and his mother had been getting reacquainted over the past year and slowly rebuilding their relationship. He'd been resistant, at first. But now he was grateful for his wife's encouragement and the second chance he and his mother had been given.

Riley's family was vacationing in Vienna. His relationship with his in-laws had improved but was far from perfect. He and Ted George had one thing in common: they both loved Riley and wanted her to be happy.

Fifteen months ago, Travis couldn't have imagined he'd be happily married and living in Asheville when he wasn't filming in LA. But now he couldn't imagine his life without the people in this room. Especially the incredible woman sitting to his right.

Riley's lovely face and warm smile were the first things he wanted to see each morning and the last things he wanted to see each night, for the rest of his life.

* * * * *

WE HOPE YOU ENJOYED
THIS BOOK FROM

*Luxury, scandal, desire—welcome to
the lives of the American elite.*

Be transported to the worlds of oil barons, family dynasties,
moguls and celebrities. Get ready for juicy plot twists,
delicious sensuality and intriguing scandal.

6 NEW BOOKS AVAILABLE EVERY MONTH!

#2833 AN HEIR OF HIS OWN
Texas Cattleman's Club: Fathers and Sons
by Janice Maynard
When Cammie Wentworth finds an abandoned baby, the only man who can help is her ex, entrepreneur Drake Rhodes. Drake isn't looking to play family, but as the sparks burn hotter, will these two find their second chance?

#2834 WAYS TO WIN AN EX
Dynasties: The Carey Center • by Maureen Child
Serena Carey once wanted forever with hotelier Jack Colton, but he left her brokenhearted. Now he's back, and she, reluctantly, needs his help on an event that could make her future—she just has to resist the chemistry that still sizzles between them...

#2835 JUST FOR THE HOLIDAYS...
Sambrano Studios • by Adriana Herrera
The last man casting director Perla Sambrano wants to see is Gael Montez. But the handsome A-lister is perfect for her new show. When they're snowed in during a script reading, will he become the leading man in her heart just in time for Christmas?

#2836 THE STAKES OF FAKING IT
Brooklyn Nights • by Joanne Rock
The daughter of a conman, actress Tana Blackstone has put her family's past and the people they hurt, like Chase Serrano, behind her. But when Chase needs a fake fiancée, she can't refuse. Soon, this fake relationship reveals very real temptation...

#2837 STRICTLY CONFIDENTIAL
The Grants of DC • by Donna Hill
With her family's investments in jeopardy, Lexi Randall needs the help of real estate developer Montgomery Grant, who just happens to also be a notorious playboy. When the professional turns *very* personal, can she still save the family business—and her heart?

#2838 SECRETS, VEGAS STYLE
by Kira Sinclair
Cultivating his bad-boy reputation, nightclub CEO Dominic Mercado uses it to help those in need and keep away heartbreak. But when his best friend's sister, Meredith Forrester, who's always been off-limits, gets too close, their undeniable attraction may risk everything...

*The last man casting director Perla Sambrano wants
to see is Gael Montez. But the handsome A-lister is
perfect for her new show. Now, snowed in during a
script reading, will he become the leading man in
her heart just in time for Christmas?*

Read on for a sneak peek at
Just for the Holidays…
by Adriana Herrera.

"Sure, why don't you tell me how to feel, Gael, that's always
been a special skill of yours." She knew that was not the
way they would arrive at civility, but she was tired of his
sulking.

She could see his jaw working and a flush of pink
working up his throat. She should leave this alone. This
could not lead anywhere good. She'd already felt what his
touch did to her. Already confirmed that the years and the
distance had done nothing to temper her feelings for him,
and here she was provoking him. Goading an answer out
of him that would wreck her no matter what it was. And he
would tell her because Gael had never been a coward. And
he'd already called her bluff once today.

He moved fast and soon she was pressed to a wall or a
door, she didn't really care, because all of her concentration
was going toward Gael's hands on her. His massive, rock-
hard body pressed to her, and she wished, really wished, she
had the strength to resist him. But all she did was hold on
tighter when he pressed his hot mouth to her ear.

"I've told myself a thousand times today that I'm not supposed to want you as much as I do." He sounded furious, and if she hadn't known him as well as she did, she would've missed the regret lacing his words. He gripped her to him, and desire shot up inside her like Fourth of July fireworks, from her toes and exploding inside her chest.

"Wouldn't it be something if we could make ourselves want the things that we can have," she said bitterly. He scoffed at that, and she didn't know if it was in agreement or denial of what she'd said. It was impossible to focus with his hands roaming over her like they were.

"I don't want to talk about it." *It. I* and *T*. She had no idea what the *it* even was. It could've been so many things. His father's abandonment, their love story that had been laid to waste. The years they had lost, everything they could never get back. Two letters to encompass so much loss and heartbreak. It was on the tip of her tongue to demand answers, to push him to stop hiding, to tell her the truth for once. But she could not make herself speak, the pain in his eyes stealing her ability to do so.

He ran a hand over his head, like he didn't know where to start. Like the moment was too much for him, and for a moment she thought he would actually walk away, leave her standing there. He kissed her instead.

Don't miss what happens next in…
Just for the Holidays…
by Adriana Herrera,
the next book in her new Sambrano Studios series!

Available November 2021 wherever
Harlequin Desire books and ebooks are sold.

Harlequin.com